I0547180

ABOVE THE ETHER - 3RD GATE

2nd Edition

YEMISI AREMU OTASANYA

ISBN: 9785315991

ISBN-13: 978-9785315998 (Johnny Jes

Limited)

Published & Printed in Nigeria by:

2nd Edition republished on the 29th May 2024

Johnny Jes Limited,

Durosinmi Street, Off George Street, Somolu,
Lagos.
Tel: +234-1-8794566; +234-813-665-6018
e-mail: johnnyjes12@gmail.com;
johnnjes@yahoo.com;
yemisiaremu@gmail.com

All Rights Reserved:

DEDICATION

To the Lord, the Creator, the one and only true Lord, who gave me the insight for the content of this book, and life and health to write it.

CONTENT

ACKNOWLEDGMENTS

I hereby acknowledge my ever-faithful husband, who took time to read each and every word, and encouraged me to finish this book. My lovely children, Tomi and Tolu, gave me some ideas for this book. My loving and caring mom, believed in me. My siblings, Toyin, Abiodun, and Ayo, believed in me and gave great encouragement. My Kenyan friend, Edna, said that my words were inspiring and encouraged me to pick up my writing pen again. My boss, Chris, did not mind my pursuing of this passion while working. My colleagues, Davies and Obinna, gave me cover design ideas. My Israeli friend, Sharon, also inspired my writing. My mentor, Mr. Clem, always has time to edit my books. My colleague and friend, Chigo, told me that I should start writing again. My dad, whose soul I pray rests in perfect peace, was a great inspiration, as well as to all of humanity whom I believe will one day find true love and joy.

PROLOGUE

The climate was becoming unpredictable fast, and meteorologists from around the world could no longer forecast the weather. The United Nations had called for a global meeting with all world leaders to address climate change and massively destructive natural disasters. CASA told them that human activities were the direct cause of drastic climate change. But Batu knew better. He was the M.D. of CASA and the prince of Pitaluna, a royal kingdom in a dimension under the Earth known as PIT. The Earth was falling fast and becoming more violent and unpredictable. Everything would change: the climate, the people, and all else.

It had been almost 6,000 years since the invasion by the Pitalunians. PIT promised gifts of knowledge, and the Earth had advanced in technology, but the Earth was falling and falling fast. At every four-red moon, the Earth passed through another gate. Red was the sign of doom. Earth had never ascended, and thus, its inhabitants did not know the sign of ascension.

A long time ago, before the invasion, the first man was King of the Earth, sea, and over everything below the sea. The Omega made and beautified him, and the Earth's position was at the first gate from Heaven. Madu loved this place. It was beautiful indeed. The air was unpolluted. The sky was the brightest of blue. It was perfect. Madu's first assignment as King was to master the Earth. He was to be fruitful, multiply, replenish the Earth, subdue it, have dominion over other creatures upon the Earth, and understand the ways of the land, sea, and air.

These were blessings that could also turn into curses. They were the first set of rules given to mankind.

"How would I turn these blessings into curses? How do I claim all these blessings for myself and send him to the very ends of the pit?" thought Saturnia, the King of PIT.

The great Dracon powered on his computer with a thought. A massive beam of light suddenly emerged from the once-blank wall before him. It shimmered, and an image appeared on the screen. On his right sat a beautiful woman. Her straight, long white hair covered her head with two perfect braids, encircling it beneath an azurite gemstone crown. The Queen of PIT looked at the image on the screen with disgust and said, "They look happy."

Dracon responded, "That will soon end. I have a plan."

He stood up from his golden throne and drank from his cup—an elixir made from PIT. Just then, Batu walked in, breathing hard like a man from battle.

"How was the race, my boy?" Dracon asked the young prince, whose white, straight, short hair glowed dimly and blue eyes were downcast. As a gesture of respect, he bowed slightly to his royal parents with his left hand to his chest.

"Not as much fun, Father," responded the prince. "Too few in attendance for my ego."

Batu clicked his fingers twice, and his helmet melted into a small chip on his right earpiece. His father picked up an azurite goblet from the glistening set to his right, offered the prince a drink, and said, "I have a plan, Batu. The creator diminished us to this PIT after crowning Madu as the Earth's ruler. We no longer receive his blessings. We now drink this elixir. I have summoned the twelve princes for a meeting at noon."

Each prince received the King's message on their electroencephalographic headset and soon assembled in the meeting room. It was a massive room, shaped like a dodecagon, with a darkly tinted azurite marble floor. The conference table in the middle of the room was a unique metal, which could change shape and move according to the programming from Dracon's mind; he was the only Pitalunian who had access to control it. Aside from the table, there were twelve golden giant statues of Dracon at the edges of the room. The twelve princes occupied their positions at the table but remained standing. The deep reverberating sound of a horn filled the room, and the King of PIT walked in.

All heads slightly but quickly bowed in respect, and fear was visible on the faces of most of the princes. Dracon shapeshifted into the form of a fearsome dragon, his favorite. The whole room quaked, and there was thundering as he approached the crowd of twelve royal bloodlines. The shapeshifter sat on the outstretched palm of a more miniature dragon statue, which the table fashioned at his approach. He transformed into another figure, and a cloak of darkness was about him. He tapped a green button on the six-inch-wide keyboard engraved on the tail of the dragon statue, which also was the single armrest of his chair. A low humming sound rose from the unique metal's surface, and twelve chairs emanated from the sides of the table, where each prince stood. They all sat down without making the slightest sound. An image of the surface of the Earth immediately appeared two feet above the middle of the table.

"My adversary is there. It was he who changed our fate. You all know what I want. Tell me how to achieve this feat," said Dracon, looking at the image that filled the holographic screen.

One of the princes began to speak. It was Subtila, the prince of trickery. He was 6'2" feet tall with coffee-brown eyes, straight, long, dark-brown hair, and slightly pointed ears. His hugely perfect frame did not reveal his mastery of trickery, for one would easily trust his humble and innocent gaze. That was part of his art; none on PIT could beat him at trickery. He was the master of deception before the cast-down.

"My Lord and King: once beautiful and perfect, but now fearsome and grim. You are truly unbeatable if not for the appearance of Madu."

Dracon took no offense. If someone had something wise to say, it was Subtila. He always started his conversations with jest and was well-known for this. Even Dracon's always terrible side never showed up whenever Subtila gave a speech.

Subtila continued, "I have studied Madu. He is a truly perfect and wise man. He is supposed to ascend to the final gate, and then he can rule over us," he exclaimed. "Ahhh! I won't bore you with details of what you already know. But, if you can grant me some more of your time," he said and paused momentarily. "He communes with Omega. He has access to the great above. Thus, if Dracon may permit me to suggest..."

"Straight to the point," barked Dracon.

"We could make him go blind," said Subtila.

At first, there was silence in the massive room. Then, a deep throaty grunt, which got louder, resounded and was followed by a loud burst of laughter—the room filled with fire. Dracon was laughing. The princes dared not laugh.

"Are you joking?" Dracon asked. The laughter suddenly stopped and was replaced by an angry tone. "Make him blind, and then what?" he asked the prince.

"And then, my King, he would lose everything if he cannot see anything. When we put him to sleep, and while sleeping, we change everything he has known. We take his true memories away, and only lies become his truth. Then, his generations would never know the truth, and Earth would fall here: into this Kingdom. We can have plenty to drink for all eternity. We will have the great harvest from his seed and generations."

Another prince spoke up. He bowed slightly. He was Knowbilia, the prince of PIT knowledge. He was the custodian of knowledge of all that has been and will be. Though a lot has been re-written since he was displaced, Dracon had approved the funds for a research project to find out about things that would occur in the future. His time machine project, the machine that would take them to the past and the future, was used to document the events that had happened or would happen. However, it has been unsuccessful so far. But the funds kept coming, and the project continued.

"How are you going to make a perfect man sleep deep enough for you to take his memory?" asked Knowbilia, directing a stern gaze at Subtila.

"Madu is knowledgeable in all things. In physical strength, he is non-comparable. In vigor and excellence, he is non-lacking. Are you going to play him a symphony? Or sing him a lullaby? More so, how are you going to access the surface of the Earth? Nothing from PIT can go there. Not even 10 miles below the surface can be assessed by any being from PIT," said Knowbilia while gesturing at the other princes to agree with him. All the other princes nodded in silent agreement.

"We are going to plant a virus," responded Subtila in defense. "There is a spot of weakness through which we can plant this virus. All we need is the perfect hologram to extend physical Earth and make it appear to continue over the Great Gorge. Once Madu's curiosity can get him to venture further than the ends of the Earth, he would fall into the tar, putting him to sleep. We then can take his memory."

On Earth, Madu strolled around his home. He had explored this part of Earth before, but it looked different from his last visit. An azurite mountain loomed far ahead of him.

"What is this element I can see far ahead? Eva, what do you think? I have not seen such on the Earth before," asked Madu, speaking to the woman beside him.

Eva gazed at the mountain for a long time and said, "It's not so magnificent, though."

She wore a white linen short-sleeve shirt that stopped just above the waistline of her white linen trousers. Madu wore a longer shirt and trousers to match.

"I would like to explore further," Madu said as he held her right hand and pulled her gently towards him. He looked deep into her colorless and clear glass eyes.

"I am coming with you," she said with a tone he could not argue.

Madu knew Eva would not have left him, even if he had insisted. Whenever he saw something that could threaten them and wanted to explore, she followed. But Madu had a strange feeling about the mountain and preferred she waited for him beside the sycamore tree. Nevertheless, he did not argue and went towards the unknown with her, holding her hand firmly as they approached the new scene with bold steps. Neither of them spoke for the duration of the trek. Earth had no jagged-edged, dangerous mountains, rocks, or hills at the time. It was impossible to fall and get hurt or die from climbing because the Earth quickly leaned over to cushion one's fall.

They reached the base of the mountain. Its brilliance was so intense, but their crystal glass eyes were not the least affected. Madu held onto Eva's hand still. He took a step closer to the looming azurite and fell. It was so sudden and unexpected that the jerk pulled Eva along. They fell through space. It was pitch-black. The glass and transparent pupil of their eyes took in the darkness and turned dark brown. He became afraid for the first time. He heard a chilling scream nearby. It was Eva's voice, but he could not see her. They had been falling for a very long time.

"Eva!" he called out to her. She kept screaming.

"Eva! Can you hear me? I am right here," he said, as he swayed his hands frantically towards the direction of her voice in mid-air, trying to reach her.

The screaming suddenly stopped. Madu felt so desperate and helpless. Unexpectedly, his body hit something cold and hard. He fainted, but only for a moment. A cold substance started to creep over his body. It was all over his legs and thighs. Then, it covered his torso and chest. He felt an acidic taste on his tongue as it entered his mouth, nose, and ears. He lost consciousness.

An electric jolt woke Madu up. Pale white hands pulled him from the tar. He tried to struggle, but his muscles did not bulge. As he felt his body lift off the cold floor, he also saw white hands lifting Eva. He could not speak or do anything.

Prince Knowbilia had completed exchanging Madu and Eva's real memories with false ones at PIT. Now contaminated with the virus, their bodies looked nothing like they used to. Using a sharp double-edged knife, Knowbilia made a slight cut through Madu's wrist, missing his vein. Red blood gushed out and thickened after a few minutes, but the wound did not heal.

"Great! My work here is done," exclaimed Knowbilia with a sly smile. He briefly looked at the sleeping humans and did a PIT dance as he approached the exit door.

The laboratory was pure brilliant white, and the captured kept drifting in and out of their slumber.

CHAPTER 1

THE DREAMS

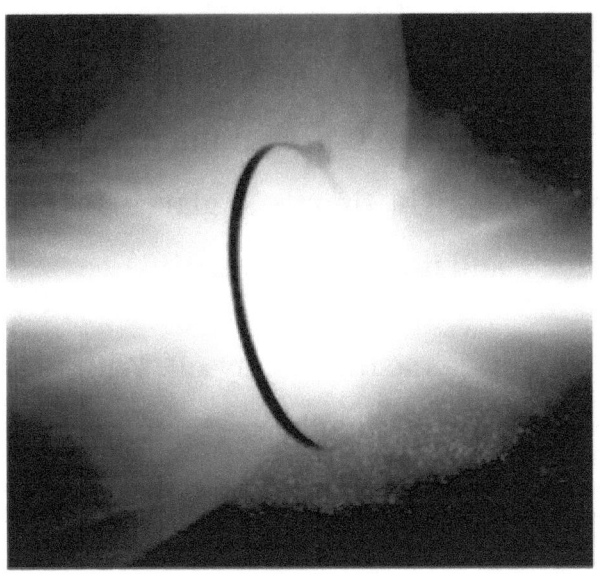

1

It was 5,900 years after the creation. The rainy season had started, and the flooding was worse this year. The rain never seems to stop falling. Diamond had to stay indoors for yet another week. Her twins were almost bored to death. She picked up the T.V. remote from the bamboo table in the living room and pressed the power–button with her right thumb. A glance at the wall clock, and it was 8:00 p.m.

"Finally, some time to myself. With the kids asleep, I can finally rest and have some personal mommy time," she thought.

A familiar Nokia tune began to buzz from inside her pocket.

"That's Jim," she said to no one in particular. Her husband was a telecom engineer working as a consultant in Abu Dhabi.

"Hello, Dia. How are you today?" Jim said in his calm, baritone voice, using the nickname he called her by.

They talked for about an hour. Diamond tried to stifle a yawn that wouldn't go away. Her body stretched out on the green leather couch. She blew goodnight kisses into the phone but was too tired to do much else; she staggered to their shared bedroom and was immediately asleep. It was darker than usual outside. The sky was starless, and everything 100 meters away from Diamond's house was sleeping, except for a white, undistinguishable figure standing by the fenced building wall. A gentle breeze blew the curtain of the open bedroom window. The vintage Cesibius' Clepsydra wall clock chimed twice. It was 2:00 a.m.

The vision in her head was hazy. The night sky was dark and cloudy. Diamond was in her green nighty, washing the dishes. The twins were asleep. A shadow crept behind her and hugged her. It was Jim.

"You smell like vanilla, my love," said Jim as he kissed the nape of her neck.

Diamond was happy to have him back. She missed him so much. Jim suddenly stopped holding her.

"Is something burning?" he asked.

Diamond did not hear him. Her eyes were on the massive ball of fire approaching them from the night sky. She screamed.

"Jim! It has started."

The massive ball fell out of sight, and a loud explosion followed. The ground shook. Jim ran to the twins' room as if programmed to know what to do in this particular situation. Diamond followed, running closely behind him. He lifted and carried the sleeping boy while she seized Daisy. They ran out of the house towards the mountain a few miles away. The ground cracked open with a loud hiss, and thick black smoke emanated from within. Huge gulps of flowing lava spewed out and mixed with saturated ground from the non-ceasing rain.

"We must hurry, Jim," shouted Diamond.

There was chaos and confusion all over. People were running and screaming. The ground opened to their right and swallowed some men in white lab coats. They had been in an argument before their doom. She had heard their conversation: "How can you say you did not see it coming until it was too late?" one of them had asked while struggling through the flooded thicket.

The other man kept crying as he responded.

"It had already gotten here with about an hour of impact left before we saw it. It was invisible and black until it reached us."

"Oh, God!" said the first man that spoke.

Diamond knew they were from C.A.S.A. She and her family ran through the thicket and a muddy path towards the mountain. The lava was gaining on them. They got to the mountain's base and climbed through the upward-winding pathway. The lava had surrounded the mountain. They got to the top. The lava had stopped increasing just as it was about to reach the top.

Diamond woke up with a scream, all covered in sweat. It was only a dream. One year after the first dream, Diamond had another dream. It was March 2011.

She was on the seashore, looking out to sea. A huge wave was coming towards her. It destroyed everything. She saw the earth fall through a massive gate inscribed with the word 'ETA.'

She woke up trembling all over. That morning, Sky News reporter Helen Stuart read the headline:

"An undersea mega-thrust 9.0 earthquake just struck off the coast of Tohoku, Japan; it has triggered a powerful tsunami."

The images on the television screen were frightful. A brief flash of her dream the previous night exploded in her mind. It was as if she was having the dream all over again. She could see the waves coming, their height towering up to heaven. Ding dong! The sound of the doorbell jolted her back to reality. She looked at the wall clock. It was 6:30 a.m. She shook her head from side to side as if to clear her thoughts.

"That must be the milkman," she said aloud and opened the front door. No one was there, just a pint of milk in a transparent glass bottle. She picked it up and closed the door gently. It was drizzling slightly outside, as expected. The rain was not as much this year, and the kids had two more weeks before their final exams. Diamond quickly made some pancakes with pepperoni sauce and checked the time. It was 7:00 a.m. Someone tapped her legs from behind. It was David.

"Mommy, are we going to school today?" he asked. "Yes, my love. You guys are going to school today," she replied and planted kisses on both cheeks. He still looked sleepy.

"I don't feel like going to school today, mom. School is so boring," said David.

"So, who would babysit you, my dear? You know I have to go to work today," his mother responded.

"No, Mom. I hate school," said David.

"Okay. But today is your taekwondo class. Don't you like taekwondo?" his mother asked.

"Taekwondo is also boring. Mommy, I love chess. Only chess," cried David.

"Alright. That's fine. But, do go to school today. Mommy will be so happy with you and give you tons of kisses." She planted numerous kisses on both cheeks. The boy seemed happy and agreed to go to school.

"Mommy! I'm awake."

A female voice, full of the sound of yawning, interrupted. It was Daisy.

"Great! Let's have our morning devotion and prepare for school," said Diamond to her children.

··

At C.A.S.A. headquarters, Blanton was already at the lab as early as 7:00 a.m. EDT, observing the most recent photographs sent in by Ammag, the low-orbit space telescope. It was the image of an eerie white star in the middle of what seemed to look like a gaseous pyramid structure. The star appeared to be seated right on the pyramid's apex and embedded into it. It was named Star HD 44179. He observed the following image: a flying star with a translucent gaseous frame of wings named "Hen 2 – 437," a planetary nebula that resided in the Milky Way with about 3,000 others like it. Blanton was angry. He clearly remembered the other images he had seen Batu staring at in his office two nights before. His mind went through the events that had happened that night.

He had planned to close early that night so as to get enough sleep after not sleeping for the past three nights. He had already stepped out of the building and clocked out at 8:00 p.m. Upon reaching his car, he realized that he had forgotten his catadioptric telescope.

"I'll just take my secret passageway," he murmured, smiling mischievously and cheerfully to himself. He snuck into the secret passage that had always been there, even before the C.A.S.A. building's construction. He had gone to the store to pick up the telescope when, due to fatigue and carelessness, he hit his head against the side drawer and landed on the hard floor, knocked out.

That night, Batu logged into the building's security system from his office to check that everyone had clocked out. "Yes. They all had," he said, whispering to the empty office and pressing a button on his watch. A light beam shot forth from its screen, and a holographic image became visible. It was a recent image captured by Ammag 2, the space telescope in a high elliptical orbit. A replica of Ammag was positioned in low earth orbit, but Ammag 2 had a higher DPI. An image of the massive holographic machine projecting stellar graphics onto the earth filled the center of Batu's office.

He quickly observed that Orion seemed out of place, and two bright stars were too close for comfort. One of the UFO holograms kept fading in and out, and it was altogether beginning to dissipate.

"This won't take longer than a few seconds," thought Batu.

Back in the store, Blanton had begun to stir. He tried to sit upright but felt dizzy. He leaned his back on the wall for support. He shook his head to clear it and remembered what had brought him there. He looked at his watch.

"Wow! 2:00 a.m.," he quietly exclaimed.

Quickly grabbing the unwrapped telescope set, he got up, approached the only door to the storeroom, and opened it. Outside was unusually dark, such that he could not see the floor. He scouted around. He could not see anything. Suddenly, a thin silvery line appeared from nowhere and touched the floor just an inch from his feet. The line continued to extend until it touched something. Another door appeared. Blanton recognized the door. It was the door to Batu's office. Blanton was in shock.

"Is this some other project I don't know about? Batu called the shots and had the reputation of not informing me until it was convenient," he thought.

It seemed as if the silvery line was pulsating. Blanton stooped down and slowly extended his left hand towards it. He touched it only slightly. Nothing happened. Gaining more confidence, he touched it again. It felt smooth and hard. He had not stepped out of the store all this time. It was still very dark, and the floor remained unseen. Blanton glided his palm across where the floor should have been. His palm dropped into space, and his weight plummeted into darkness. In shock but quickly recovering and with quick reflexes, he grabbed the silvery line with his right hand and hoped it was strong enough to hold him. The thin line felt warm and alive, with its pulse beating against his fist. He breathed a deep sigh of relief and held fast with his second hand, struggling to pull his weight back into the storeroom. His heartbeat widened in his chest, and he sat on the floor of the room, staring into the darkness that would have consumed him some moments ago.

"There was supposed to be a floor there," he thought. A strange symphony started to play at the end of the silvery line from Batus' office door. Blanton listened.

"Where had he heard that sound before?" the scientist wondered as the sound got louder. He felt drawn to it. At the end of the line, Batu's door began to vibrate and became translucent. Blanton picked up his telescope and hung it across his shoulders. He would walk on the line to the translucent door and confront Batu about this new project he was unaware of. The scientist started to walk on the line to the opposite door with both hands stretched out for balance. Strangely enough, he felt at one with the line. He could feel the pulse of the line merging with his heartbeat. The air was very static and had an electric feel to it.

Now, at the other door, he touched the handle and was immediately transfixed into a trance; his body became instantly frozen. Part of him stepped out of his body and walked through the door. He saw a massive holographic image of the Earth's elliptical orbit superimposed on the Earth's lower orbit. The image came from Batu's watch, who did not see him. He was back in his body outside the door in a split second. His body unfroze, and losing his balance, he fell into the gorge below. Batu turned towards the door at the same instance; he thought he had heard a sound. He had shrugged his shoulders and continued, fixated on the repairs.

Blanton had woken up in the storeroom with a headache. The event of the past few minutes seeped into his mind immediately and with such clarity that his head throbbed hard.

"How did he get back here? Was it all an illusion that resulted from hitting his head?" he wondered.

He remembered the gorge and staggered to his feet to open the door. It led toward the corridor from which he had snuck into the building. Amazed and confused, he snuck back out with his telescope still across his shoulders but completely forgotten. The next day, he took a day off for a medical check-up.

The alarm from his watch rang, bringing his mind back to the present. It was time for the lecture he had been invited to at the Massachusetts Institute of Technology.

....

That very same day, on the other side of the world in West Africa, Diamond got to the office a little earlier than usual. The outskirt traffic was unexpectedly light. Diamond stretched her body length as she exited her Mitsubishi, glad she did not experience backache from the morning's drive. She hoped for the same experience when returning home in the evening. She placed her I.D. on the scanner at the front door of the building. A side screen displayed her identity and read:

Mrs. Diamond Jim. Senior Biochemist, National Institute of Pharmaceutical Research and Industrial Development.

The door clicked loudly and opened to allow her in. The system automatically clocked her in. The first thing on her mind was breakfast, and she went straight to the kitchen. The office building was quiet. No one was at the office yet except for the security and cleaners.

"Hello!" she said to one of the ladies dressed in a uniform, who seemed to be finishing her chores.

"Good morning," the lady in yellow dungaree responded.

"How was your weekend, and how is your family?" asked Diamond.

"Very well. Thanks, and yours?" the lady asked in turn. "Great!" responded Diamond as she turned towards the kitchen. She prepared a cup of hot, steaming natural cocoa and honey. The same domestic worker was now in the kitchen.

"Have you been in Abuja for long?" Diamond asked.

"Yes. I was born here," the lady responded.

"Oh! That's cool. I moved here with my parents when I was six years old. Abuja is a nice and quiet city. Great for raising a family," said Diamond.

The lady responded by smiling. Diamond smiled back. She could not get her mind off her last dream, even though she was trying to. Fortunately, the conversation temporarily freed her from the images that kept creeping up.

"My dream happened. I am amazed. How terrible!" she thought. "All those people are now dead due to the tsunami. And I only had the dream a few hours before the event. Maybe if I had the dream some days before, I might have sent a warning to Tohoku."

She remembered the live video of the tsunami from the news and the black, murky, high waves sweeping over the landscape, filled with people, cars, houses, trees, and all sorts of other things. Her mind went to the first dream in which an asteroid hit the earth, resulting in a massive global volcanic eruption. She clearly remembered the path her family took to escape the ordeal. It seemed very familiar, like where her dad took her for a family picnic when she was young.

"Hey, Diamond! Always the early bird," a voice exclaimed. It was her colleague, Linda, who cut through her thoughts.

"Oh! Hi," she responded and smiled. Her tea was already cold, and the cup was still full.

"I can see you are in deep thought. Missing Jim. Right?" Linda cajoled her.

"Yeah! Missing him," Diamond responded. Her hand was under her jaw and resting on the table.

"I can just imagine how you must feel. To be separate from your darling in this cold and wet season. Hmm?" said Linda, still teasing her.

"You are such a tease. How about, what a lovely bright day it is! Hmm?" Diamond mimicked with a naughty look on her face and asked, "Are we set for this morning's presentation?"

"Yep! I am. I need to refresh my makeup," Linda said, pulling a seat at the same table with Diamond and placing her hot steaming coffee on the table.

"I might just catch some cool dude ready to settle down for marriage at that conference. You know! Some top guns are showing up, and some are bachelors."

"I can see you have done your research," said Diamond.

"Of course. I need a "Jim" to be missing, too, you know!

"It's high time I get serious and settled," said Linda.

"Yeah!" Diamond agreed and quickly calculated her planned activities for the day: "Office, pick up the kids, buy groceries, cook, and pick up Jim. Oh! Pick up, Jim." She then spoke out loud excitedly, "Jim will be back today. Yippee!"

"You are practically blushing, girl! I'm glad you guys are still so in love after two kids. I hope my "Jim" will be cooler than your Jim," said Linda.

"I'm sure he'll be perfect for you. I have to go and tidy up some stuff for the presentation. Will you be riding with me to the conference?" asked Diamond.

"Yep! Definitely. I will not be going with the staff bus," replied Linda.

"Okay, cool. See you then," Diamond said as she picked up her green leather handbag and left the office kitchen.

....

Meanwhile, back in Massachusetts, Blanton already returned to C.A.S.A. after the lecture. He felt stupid throughout. He taught the subject ASTR 198: 'Searching Between The Stars.' His mind kept replaying the event that occurred two nights before.

"I have to go back to that storeroom, if not for anything else but for sanity's sake. Was it a dream? That must be some vivid real-life dream. Was it real? I certainly hope not. That would be too crazy," he thought.

He tried to focus on the project at hand and not make it seem obvious that his mind was on something else. Then, the intercom on the wall in the lab rang loudly. He ignored it for a while, but the ringing was persistent. He picked up the phone's remote from the laboratory table by him and pressed the speaker button. The front desk office personnel's voice boomed over the speakers. It was loud and without emotion.

"Hello, Mr. Blanton."

"Hello, Britney," responded Blanton. He immediately recognized the female voice.

"The M.D. has requested a brief meeting with you at his office," she explained.

Blanton did not answer immediately. He was used to being called in for brief meetings with Batu. It would have been usual if this had happened two nights before, but now he felt rather uneasy.

"Mr. Blanton?" she called again. The tone of her voice indicated her patience was running out.

"Yes. Thank you. I will go and see him now. Thank you," he said.

"Alright, sir. Have a lovely day," she said and dropped the call—the hang-up tone cut through the usually quiet room. Blanton hung up, also.

He prepared himself. Before two nights ago, he would have walked into Batu's Office, eager for the next project or news, but now, he let out a heavy breath, removed his lab coat, and hung it on the hanger close to the exit door. He entered the locker room and stood before the full-body-length standing mirror. Staring back at him was his image, all confident like always.

"I see no need to worry here. It was only a dream," he said to his image and left the lab.

Batu stood by the glass window, looking down at the busy streets of the city. The C.A.S.A. building was the second tallest in Massachusetts, towering up to 235 meters. At just 5.8 meters less than the John Hancock building, it was almost the tallest building in the city.

There was a gentle knock at the door. Batu knew who it was. People only came into his Office if summoned. Using voice control, he spoke to the building: "Open door."

A female robotic voice responded, "Opening door for Mr. Blanton."

Batu was now facing the door. Blanton walked in as boldly and emotionless as he could.

"Good day, Batu."

Batu looked at him for a while without first responding. "Take your seat," he said some seconds later.

"I was told you called in sick. Are you effective now?" Batu asked, examining the scientist with his deep blue eyes.

Blanton sat on an opposite chair, trying to look composed. He had always wondered why Batu used that phrase when he wanted to learn how someone was faring.

"I'm effective," replied Blanton.

This usually ended with everyone in the conversation laughing because it was a funny, rare phrase used only by the M.D.

"That's good to know. Have you gone through the recent images sent in by Ammag?" asked Batu. His white full hair looked illuminated by the sun's rays that passed through the glass window into the room. His blue eyes stared at the images. Blanton's eyes followed his gaze. The M.D. pressed a button on his desk, and the images were displayed on the large LCD on the wall opposite his desk. Blanton swirled the chair around to face the screen.

"Yes. Saw them two nights ago," he answered.

"And are you not excited, Blanton? You don't seem excited!"

He walked towards the screen and continued talking, gesturing like a professor with an exciting discovery to share with his students.

"Of all the images we have received so far, this is the most exciting," explained Batu.

He waved his hands, and the screen displayed image after image. He paused at image seven, a red triangle with a star embedded between two gaseous pyramid structures.

"Isn't that amazing? We should share this with the world." Batu waved his hand again, and the remote sensor on his middle finger switched the slides on the screen. He stopped at the 13th image. The spectacularly symmetrical wings of Hen 2-437 showed a magnificent blue hue. Batu looked at Blanton, who quickly tried to look excited.

"Yes!" Blanton said, now standing up. "That one particularly intrigued me. It is amazing. The world needs to see these images, and we need to even reach further to the stars," said Blanton.

"My exact thoughts. So, we are good. Write up your script and let me have it by tomorrow evening," Batu said, glancing at his watch.

"Lunchtime already? Wow! Care to join us for lunch? I'm meeting my wife at L'Espalier."

"I'm good, sir. I would like to quickly round up some stuff and get started on the script right away," Blanton said, politely declining the invite.

"Always so hardworking," Batu said to the half-German, half-British scientist. "You know you are still the best scientist to date. I hope you can keep that up for a long time."

Blanton nodded as he turned to leave and said, "I hope so, too."

....

Meanwhile, Diamond was already back home in Abuja. She had completed three planned activities for the day and quickly mentally ticked off her accomplishments.

"Time to go to the open market," she said, glancing at the wall clock. It read 5:00 p.m. GMT.

"Kids!" she called at the twins glued to the T.V. watching Teletubbies.

"I have to dash to the market near the house quickly. I will be back in 20 minutes."

She waited for their response. None came. She called out again.

"Kids!"

"Okay, mom. We heard you," they responded in unison, not turning their attention away from the T.V.

Diamond quickly dashed out the door. She checked to ensure it was closed outside, and the kids could only open it inside the house.

"Don't open the door for anyone else," she said with her face pressed to the net of the parlor window from outside the flat.

"Alright, mom!" the twins answered still in unison. Their mom smiled and turned toward the market as her phone rang. Jim's ringtone: "Hello, love. I'm already at the airport," he said.

"I'm so glad you're back, love. I was supposed to pick you up," she replied in a guilt-filled tone.

"I know; it's been a hectic day for you, my love, and the conference took longer than expected. I'll take an airport taxi."

"Oh! That's great love. Thanks for your understanding. On my way to the open market. See you soon."

"Yeah! Can't wait to see you guys, also," Jim said, ending the call.

Diamond wondered if he was upset about her not picking him up from the airport as earlier planned. She hoped he wasn't. The market was only two minutes away, and Diamond was already there when she finished speaking with her husband. A quick pick of what was needed, and she was done. Walking back towards the house and climbing down a hilly road that led away from the market, Diamond noticed how blue and bright the sky was for an evening, and thought of how unusual it appeared. Standing on the hilly road for a moment to admire the glowing evening sky, two nearby mountains in the line of her sight caught her attention. The further one she recognized was the one her family went on vacation during her childhood. The other one was unknown. Both stood alone, separated from the mountain range that surrounded the city.

"Wow! This would make a lovely landscape picture for my screen saver. I can take a nice picture from right here," thought Diamond as she brought out her phone.

The phone's camera zoom lens brought the view closer. She noticed a winding pathway leading toward the second mountain she had not visited. It encircled it from the base and disappeared somewhere in the middle. The path looked very familiar.

"Where did I see that pathway?" she asked as she zoomed closer.

"Oh my God! The dream!"

She remembered running with her family on the same winding pathway through the mountain with no name and navigating around it to get to another mountain. The same mountain where she and her family were saved stood before her eyes. Her breathing increased sharply, and she became frightened. She ran home like a scared child.

Diamond got home and knocked on the door. With deep breaths, she was able to compose herself and called out to the twins, who chanted excitedly on hearing their mother's voice.

"Mommy, you stayed longer," said David.

"I'm Sorry, my love," Diamond said as she entered the house and shut the door behind her.

"Daddy called when he got to the local airport and should arrive home any minute. I have to cook fast."

"What's for dinner, Mom?" asked Daisy.

"Pounded yams and egusi soup, your dad's favorite."

"Yippee!" exclaimed David.

"I want pounded yam and egusi, too," he said.

"Not to worry. We are all having pounded yam and egusi soup for dinner," Diamond said as the kids followed her to the kitchen.

"Meanwhile, come and give your mommy a helping hand."

"Okay, Mom," they both responded at the same time. "This is a much-needed distraction," she thought as she prepared the dinner with the twins.

Jim was so happy to be back in Nigeria. His job required so much travel. He missed his twin's happy faces and could not wait to make love to his beautiful wife. He understood how tiresome combining work and caring for the twins could be. He didn't mind having to board a local taxi. The cab taxied towards Jim's house. It was a rented building with three flats and a penthouse at the top. He had always wondered how the architect created such a weird design. He called it the floating penthouse. Jim paid off the driver and walked through the gate towards his flat.

Diamond was already done cooking and had set the dining table with steaming and hot pounded yam, served with freshly cooked egusi soup and goat meat; it was a well-loved local diet.

David had been peeping out through the parlor window as soon as his mom had finished cooking, anxiously awaiting his dad's arrival. He was the first to see his father, and he screamed excitedly.

"Daddy is back, everyone!"

The twins ran to the front door to be the first to open it and give the first hug. It became a struggle. Their dad could hear the battle, and he tried to calm them. Diamond quickly left the dining table and ran to the front door. She was able to pacify the excited twins and open the door. Both twins jumped on their dad. They were so happy to see him after his six weeks in Abu Dhabi.

"Welcome home, sweetheart," said Diamond with a happy smile.

Jim hugged everyone all at once. He was so happy to see his family.

After dinner and with the kids asleep, Diamond stood between the open doors of her cupboard. She was in a dilemma between wearing her pink or green nightwear. Jim was in the shower. She unwittingly remembered that she wore the green nightwear in the dream where an asteroid struck the Earth. She decided against this and chose the polka-dotted pink one instead. Jim grabbed her right hand and in a fast turn, she was in his arms. He looked into her coffee-brown eyes and kissed her passionately. They made love almost throughout the night.

Exactly at 2:00 a.m., Diamond had another dream.

She was outside their house, standing in an open field on a night with a clear, starless sky above. It was as if she could see almost everyone in the world watching the same T.V. show, and they were really enjoying it. She could also see other pictures on the screen that were not obvious to everyone else. Some strange-looking men were chanting out spells, and everyone watching T.V. was doing exactly as they were told; they repeated the words they were commanded to repeat by the strange men. No one was aware that they did this except for Diamond. At the same time, she knew that by the time the men were done with the chants, everyone's free will would become subdued, and they would be like robots totally under the men's' control. Suddenly, the men stopped chanting and stared at her. She was the only one that did not repeat the chant. They stretched their lean bodies out of the T.V. and tried to grab her. She ran. She began to ascend some invisible steps with the men still in desperate pursuit. The steps lead directly to the sky, and as she reached the top, her head touched the ceiling. She looked up in surprise and stretched her free hand towards the sky. It felt solid, but she could not see what she touched. The sky was still before her eyes and looked continuous. The men were very close now. She hit the sky several times and was able to break through the invisible wall. She climbed through the opening and was immediately in another world. The men followed. She continued climbing through another set of invisible *steps until she reached another barrier and did the same thing. This continued until she reached a ninth world. She looked behind her but did not see the lean men. In pursuit was a very powerful celebrity and actor, whom she admired in reality. In this world, she saw bald and naked giant men with pale skin having canal relationships with men from Earth. These Earth men that were in canal relationships were only from the elite. Diamond was so afraid from the activities occurring in that world. The celebrity reached her and tried to grab her leg. She gave a mighty blow to the hard surface and broke through to yet another realm. In this realm, there were no more invisible steps.*

She could not see anyone in pursuit. She was all alone. It was very dark, and the clouds looked frightening and menacing. She was on a massive mountain with a vast, unending plateau. She suddenly understood that all the worlds were under this plateau, and Earth was under several worlds that held her in captivity. There was no space or universe, just an illusion and a prison. It was also freezing, and there was nowhere to go. She took a step forward and almost fell off the plateau's edge. Diamond was overwhelmed with so much despair and was at a loss. Suddenly, the dark, menacing clouds approached her all at once. She felt their intention. "Throw her off the cliff," they said. A gentle voice told her to believe and jump.

The clouds were almost touching her. Diamond closed her eyes and jumped. She believed that she was in the hands of whatever must have brought her here. A white-winged horse appeared and caught her in mid-air. It flew her fast to a beautiful green land, which no man could go unless chosen. The sky was more blue and brighter than anything she had seen. The color was so intense, clear, and beautiful. The grasses were green and silky, and it felt smooth under her foot as she stepped off the flying horse. Her right foot touched the field. There was a fiery golden city in front of her. She looked back at where she had come from and became suddenly frightened. The dark clouds had also crossed over to the beautiful plains and were still in pursuit. Diamond ran for her life. She knew if she was caught, she would be dead on Earth. She ran towards the city and towards the only giant gate that led into the city. It was shut, but she still ran towards it. The clouds were so fast. Diamond wanted to cry.

"They are not supposed to be able to reach me here. How could they have crossed the gorge?" she thought in panic.

As she reached the gate, the clouds got to her and were about to envelop her when the gate sprang open. There were blinding lights, and she was pulled in by a man's hand.

Diamond woke up.

....

Blanton was also awake. It was 9:00 p.m. in Massachusetts, five hours ahead of Nigeria, and he had planned to clock out so he could sneak back into the building to confirm his previous experience; otherwise, he would just go mad. He got to the storeroom as intended and was careful not to hit his head.

"If this same thing happens again, maybe I'll finally go crazy," Blanton thought as he waited for five more hours until 2:00 a.m.

Batu checked to see if everyone had clocked out as usual. He had been summoned to P.I.T. for a brief meeting with Dracon. "Yes. Everyone had clocked out," he said, staring at his laptop screen.

He pressed a button on his desk, and the wall behind his chair became transparent. It moved like a wall of gelatinous substance. Batu put his hand through first, paused momentarily, and then walked into the wall.

It was now 2:00 a.m. Blanton opened the door of the storeroom. His heart was beating fast. He heard a soft hum. The silver lining was right there. Also, there was a deep gorge below. He gasped and stepped back into the storeroom. Opposite him and at the end of the silver line was the wall of Batu's Office, which was as transparent as before. He took five deep breaths and stood up. He crossed the gorge safely and was soon at the opposite door. He again touched the handle, and another part of him was quickly in Blanton's Office. Batu was standing in front of an open portal, about to enter. He was behind a gelatinous sort of wall. Blanton approached the wall and touched it. His hand went through. He stepped in with his right leg, and it went through. He pushed his whole body in and was now face to face with Batu. No reaction came from the M.D. The man did not see him nor sense his presence. Blanton was amazed. Batu stepped into the portal, and Blanton followed. They were in a sort of white metallic transparent beehive. It was very dark outside. Blanton wondered why Batu could not see him.

The beehive began to drop down fast. The speed of the drop increased until it became faster than the speed of light. Batu saw them pass through a gate, then another, and yet another. They suddenly stopped, and Batu stepped out through another portal. Blanton followed him, and before their eyes was a beautiful golden city. There were flying saucers and children playing around the streets. There were beautiful women whom he had not seen anything comparable to humans on Earth. It was like Earth, but a more advanced and unbelievable Earth. No one seemed to notice him. Blanton stayed close to Batu. There were creatures he had never seen before, also. He noticed something amiss about the place. There were no smiles on the faces of people. It felt gloomy and depressing. It was as if the beautiful city was wearing out. Batu approached a massive blue building, which sparkled in blinding brilliance. Guards in their thousands stood on both sides of the walkway and bowed as Batu passed amidst them. None of them noticed Blanton.

"Could it be that something is shielding me, or they just can't see me?" thought Blanton.

He suddenly felt more confident and less afraid. Batu entered the palace. His father was anxiously waiting. Blanton followed closely. Blanton noticed that the blue stone was the most dominant as if the whole palace was carved out of a single sparkling, blue gem-like mountain. It defined true royalty; he had never seen or heard of such wealth. Suddenly, the slam of the enormous palace door interrupted Blanton's thought. Dracon was staring at him. Batu wondered what his father was looking so sternly at.

"Get him!" Dracon ordered, shouting in a deep, angry tone as he waved his hand in the direction of his son.

Batu wondered what was happening and looked behind him. There was Blanton.

"Blanton! How did you get ..."

A sudden flash of lightning and brilliant white light filled the place. A flaming sword appeared, cutting Batu's words short. The light enveloped Blanton as if protecting him from the approaching monstrous guards. Dracon transformed into a great fiery dragon, equally wielding a fiery sword and engaged in battle with the bearer of the brilliant white light. Thunder and lightning ensued. It was totally blinding. Blanton saw a giant man with a sword fighting a dragon. He was enveloped in a ball of light that burnt the guards as they got closer. Suddenly, and as fast as the fight started, Blanton found himself moving faster than when he followed Batu through the beehive. He saw one gate, another gate, and yet another gate. Then, he was in his apartment with a total stranger who had a flaming sword.

"I am Igdaleah, and I'm the one that has been shielding you from being seen by Batu," the stranger said.

The scientist was back into his body, and was shaking in fear.

"Do not be afraid," Igdaleah said and touched his temple. A new surge of energy entered Blanton's body from the touch, and he felt courage.

"Where are you from and what is happening? Who is Batu, and where was that place? Who is the Dragon, and why did you come to help me? Why me?"

Igdaleah listened to all his questions and did not try to stop him. When Blanton became breathless, Igdaleah spoke up, slotting back his sword into its hold by his side.

"Listen well, Blanton, and do not weary yourself to know so many things now. All will become clear with time. But, this you must do and do now."

Blanton dropped his body heavily on the closest chair and sat down, looking confused. Igdaleah continued talking.

"The Earth is about to be brought to great desolation and destruction by those who hate her and mean no good for its inhabitants. Earth was formally above the 11th gate upon creation but is now at the 3rd gate. If things don't change, the Earth will fall to P.I.T. and burn. All humans will be harvested by P.I.T. I'm referring to Batu's home, and their blood will become food, while human souls will be damned to everlasting slavery. The signs are already here, and the increase in chaos shows it. Everyone will become hateful and evil as Earth plunges lower and lower. Earth must rise and rise now. If Earth descends through the 3rd gate, all hope will be lost because she cannot return.

"Why me?" Blanton asked, looking highly depressed.

"It does not matter why you were chosen. What matters is what you must now do," Igladeah said.

"Listen well. You must find the one who has been shown the way. Know that this one will need all the encouragement to take the path to salvation and must destroy the shield that has caused all to be blind," said Igdaleh as he began to fade.

"This person must climb through the closest gate to heaven. Only then can the illusion be broken, and the children of men will be able to make their decisions un-beguiled."

CHAPTER 2

THINGS START TO HAPPEN

2

PIT was in disarray. In nearly 7000 years, no human could guess the truth. But now, a human did not just guess the truth; he knew it and had proof. King Dracon had summoned all the princes of the kingdom.

"I need that wretched zombie wiped out. He and his family and friends. I need anything affiliated with him destroyed."

Those were the orders Dracon issued out. However, what bothered him was much more. He had transformed into a serpent, coiled up on his seat in the meeting room, and transfixed in deep thoughts. None of the princes dared interrupt. Loud thundering filled the atmosphere, and dark clouds formed a single giant tornado, which seemed to have a mind of its own, as it weaved its way through the streets of PIT and into the meeting room. It was a non-violent, inflowing tornado. It was the Aza, the legion of cloud spirits, guardian of the earth, and preventer of souls. Aza sits above the topmost plane of the Earth and prevents souls from escaping the realm of humans. The tornado filled the space below the ceiling, casting a gloomy shadow over the already downcast group. Another group of beings appeared out of the ground. These were several men that looked exactly alike, but with the grace of bionic robots. They had light brown, smooth skin with clean-shaven heads and could transform into any device. They were the Listeners.

With the assemblage of all the entities summoned, Dracon spoke,

"I am Saturnia. The Great King of the Great Field. The all-seeing one and mighty architect. I have summoned thee all, for the time has come in which man and his generations must now be vanquished. It is time for the harvest. No soul must inherit heaven. Earth itself must fall to PIT."

"Fall to PIT," said all the entities together in an echo.

"One of the blind, the deaf, the dumb, the scrawny, and the zombie has found the truth. He has become enlightened and must thus be destroyed. He is a son of man, and his name is Blanton. Here we know him by his slave code 7632," Dracon said as he waved his hand. At that moment, the meeting table once again transformed from its center, and a screen showing Blanton and his nuclear and extended family and friends was displayed before the entities.

"Make him sick. Rotten up his liver. Inflict his family with a virus. Give them fatal accidents on special days. Destroy him and bring his soul to me," commanded Dracon.

The Pitalunans responsible for the different ailments and calamities that befall humans departed to carry out the orders. "Nis!" called Dracon to the labor master. "Increase labor. Let them work till they fall to their death. Make 7632 offend. Kill him, or better yet, send someone to kill him or lose your immortality."

Nis sped off to carry out the order.

"The AZA!" Dracon called out to the gloomy cloud above their heads, "Increase the eye of the halo. I want to search for who 'the one' might be by myself."

"Band!" he called to the Lord of War. "Start the events that would lead up to the final war."

"Knowbilia! I know you have something for me. What is it?" Dracon asked the Prince of Knowledge.

"Thank you, my L..." Knowbilia started to speak but was cut short by Dracon.

"Spare me the pleasantries and present your idea," Dracon said sharply to the prince.

"We can connect electronic devices to an element in the Listeners so that conversations can be captured and stored in our Mainframe. That way, all electronic devices, including those found in households, schools, or offices; any device at all that is electronic would have this element, and we would have access to all that the individual does."

"So! Make it happen already!" Dracon commanded. "Wait!" Dracon ordered, halting Knowbilia, who was already leaving the meeting room. "I need to find a way to prevent men from receiving help from the kingdom above the 12th gate. I need all access and entrances blocked."

"We can infect all men with the virus of sleep and wipe out their memories," Knowbilia suggested.

"No. Not this time. I need the illusion heightened. Give the world a new project to fantasize about. Something that will make them doubt all they have ever believed in. Take them on a tour cruise to PIT. Make it a one-way journey to Phyton."

Diamond could not understand why she had these dreams or what they meant.

"Why should I be bothered by all these dreams?" she thought. After all, there was nothing she could do about them. She couldn't even help the Tohoku people in Japan, not to mention the whole world. No one would believe her. She laughed at this thought. How could she expect people to believe when she does not know what they mean? She can't even tell Jim. It will make no sense. There are no words to explain the dreams, as they seem out-of-this-world.

These thoughts ran through her mind as she was cleaning the house. It was the last Saturday of the month, a public environmental day declared by the Nigerian government.

"You seem lost in deep thoughts, my love! What could be so heavy on your mind this beautiful morning?" Jim said to his wife, his voice snapping her out of her thoughts as he entered the living room after tidying up their veranda. He had been observing her as he approached for about a minute and had noticed how drawn her face was.

She turned to face him and said, "Just a bit tired, love. You took away all my strength yesterday night," as she let out a naughty laugh. He was about to hug her when the twins busted in, calling out the chores they had accomplished.

"Bed made!" exclaimed David.

"Check!" said Daisy.

"Toys picked!" David said as he continued with the list.

"Check!" said Daisy.

"Wardrobe properly arranged!" said David.

"Check!" said Daisy.

"And, room swept!" David said, throwing his hands in the air as he finished his list.

"And check!" Daisy said, throwing up her hands also.

"Okay, guys. Shower!" their dad said, mimicking them.

"Not done!" their mom said, also copying the group.

"Oh!" the twins responded and ran back into the children's room to get a bath.

Jim held his wife in a soft embrace and said, "So, what's up, boo?"

She remembered the words of the cartoon character he was trying to mimic and laughed even more. "I'm cool."

"Yeah?" Jim said as he raised his eyebrows in disbelief.

"Okay. I've been having some strange dreams. But I'll tell you all about them later this evening," she said and glanced at the wall clock in the living room. "We are almost out of groceries, love, and the time set for the environment will soon be up. Let me quickly finish cleaning and getting ready for the open market."

"Those dreams must be troubling you. You quickly changed the topic," said Jim. "Just know that dreams can sometimes result from our experiences or from movies we watched. All those end-of-the-world movies you have been watching recently," he said, pausing briefly as he stared deep into her coffee-brown eyes.

Her expression turned into a frown.

"Especially the one with the asteroid that hit that guy, after which he turned into a superhero. Did I turn into a superhero in your dream?" he asked, trying to make light of the gist.

She smiled when he mentioned the superhero.

"Maybe Jim," she said. "It's 10:00 am. Let me serve breakfast so that we can go.

The couple decided to split the kids at the open market, popularly known as Wuse market. Diamond went with Daisy to buy the organic foods, while David stayed with his father, and they were to purchase beverages and toiletries. It was their end-of-the-month shopping, and they practically bought almost everything they would need for the month except stew and soup ingredients. They would need to replenish those weekly. One of Diamond's favorite things to do was stare at the sky at any time of the day or night and take pictures of things she found interesting. She looked up as usual and saw something she had never seen before. A rainbow surrounded the sun, and it was not its usually brilliant, blinding self. She wondered as she had never seen such before.

....

Back on PIT and carrying out King Dracon's decree, the Aza had set the halo closer to the Earth. That was the reason Diamond could see the rainbow around the sun. The halo was a mechanical structure in the shape of a pentagram. In its middle lay a black sun, and on its 5 apexes lay the symbolism of 5 realms. On the five bases of the triangles that made the apexes lay the symbolism of 5 other realms. These were the realms above the Earth and controlled Earth's affairs. People from different parts of the human realm also saw the halo, took several pictures, and posted them on social media.

Dracon sat in his throne room, deep in concentration. His mind was focused on the halo machine, and his body was afloat in mid-air in a double lotus pose.

"Where is he?" he asked as he searched and searched Earth for the one that would bring down the shield they had placed above Earth.

He maneuvered the halo behind the sun so as not to be seen. Its closeness, however, cast a rainbow around the sun's rim, creating an ominous shadow. Diamond quickly took a snapshot with her phone's camera.

"Mommy!" Daisy called, pulling her mother's sleeve to catch her attention. "Why does a rainbow surround the sun?"

Diamond returned the mobile phone to her blue boyfriend-jeans pocket and replied, "I don't know why love. But it's beautiful, right?"

"Yes, mom. Very beautiful. But I thought rainbows only show one part of their cycle," Daisy said, with a voice full of doubt as she stared at the weird rainbow.

"Yes," Diamond responded, looking down at Daisy and smiling. "We keep learning new things each day, love. We had better hurry before Dad and David finish faster than us ladies," she said as she rummaged through her bag. She brought out her shopping list, and they both stepped into the nearby organic vegetable store.

....

Back at Blanton's apartment in Massachusetts, the scientist was still in shock and had already drunk more than ten cups of coffee. He could not sleep, was anxious, and could not wrap his mind around the fact that his career had been based on lies, that he had been working for aliens, that the whole world was about to come crashing down, and that he had to find the person who would bring down a shield.

"Where would I begin?" he thought. He heard a beep and glanced at his table clock. It was 5:00 am. He picked up the navy blue hooded sweater he had tossed carelessly on the only chair in the room and put it on. "I have to leave immediately, but to where?" He was surprised that no police force, CIA, or FBI had been to his apartment yet. "Not even an alien," he said aloud. He grabbed his knapsack and started to throw things inside. "Maybe the Pitalunans are trying to keep things quiet and prevent doubt or suspicion. They had kept the secret from humans for so long. No single soul suspects their presence on Earth. Everyone thought that aliens were monsters with green, pale skin, blue blood, and big oval eyes or some monstrous, disgusting bug-like creatures," he said, sighing as he remembered the bug-like aliens in various movies. "What nonsense!" he said aloud and went into the basement. He grabbed his telescope, some canned food, and some stacks of cash. He had kept at least $10,000 in his basement for reasons he could not discern. Sarah, his wife, had insisted that they keep some cash in the basement just in case, and he had objected at first but later obliged. He stepped towards the stairs that led back upstairs and stopped suddenly. His feet had stepped on a part of the basement floor that produced a sound only he recognized.

Under his foot was the door to a secret tunnel. He stepped back and lifted off the rug that covered the door. He bent down and turned the combination. It produced three clicks, and the door slid open. He was about to enter the tunnel when the whole top floor exploded. The force pushed him into the tunnel and knocked him out momentarily. He became conscious almost immediately and quickly ran down the tunnel. He had inherited the house from his grandfather, a U.S. marine in his youth, and had also built the secret tunnel during his service years, without the knowledge of the government. Blanton and his brother used to run through the tunnel when they were kids. His brother had died in service to the military, and Blanton was the only one left. His mind went to his wife and two kids. They had traveled to South Africa for the holidays. Blanton's family usually went to South Africa every other year. They called it the "get-away from network". They stayed at a local cabin near the zoo, with absolutely no access to the internet.

"Thank God," he said, panting as he ran. "At least they should be safe at the cabin."

His wife Sarah, a celebrity actress, welcomed the idea at the time. Their son and daughter did not mind either because they loved the zoo and could escape from their parents' popular lives and the nonstop paparazzi hunt in Massachusetts.

The Listeners had already commenced their mission to destroy Blanton. One stood above the tunnel's entrance in the burnt apartment, invisible to the naked eye. The sirens of the local police and fire department could be heard for miles as they approached the burnt building. The opposite street was filled with neighbors who were lined up outside, with hands covering their ears, because of the confusing simultaneous blast of sirens.

A Listener jumped into the twelve-foot-deep opening of the tunnel's entrance and stood examining the underground corridor. A red beam shot forth from his eyes and scanned fifty meters away through the winding tunnel, searching for a human heartbeat, heat, and an electronic device. Nothing was detected. He increased the scan to one kilometer. Heartbeat and heat detected. In an instant, and with the speed of light, he grabbed a small animal. It squeaked only briefly and died. He flung the rat against the wall and continued his search five kilometers more.

Blanton heard a squeaking sound and the humming of electricity. He ran faster than he ever imagined he could run. The Listener detected heat again and the quick pulsating of a heartbeat. He ran in pursuit. Blanton heard the humming sound louder and closer than before. He looked back. Clouds of dust were in the air behind him. He saw something move like a flash of lightning, and the next thing he felt was a tightness in his throat and intense pain as he heard the sound of his neck bone-crushing. The Listener lifted the scientist into the air by his neck and squeezed.

Blanton struggled in mid-air. The naked man who grabbed his throat was almost a giant. Blanton could not breathe. The pain was unbearable. He tasted something wet and warm in his mouth. His blood spilled out from his mouth as life seeped out of him. He thought about his mission to find the one that would break the shield. He thought about his family. He struggled to look into the green eyes of the Listener. The Listener squeezed harder at his throat. Blanton saw darkness. He was dead. The Listener threw him to the ground and lifted his left foot to smash his brain. He read his vitals. Nothing. The man was dead. The Listener changed his mind and instead transformed into Blanton. He had read the dying man's memory and knew what to do next. He grabbed Blanton's knapsack and scanned it - a telescope, a travel ticket to South Africa, $10,000, and canned food with no nutrient value. He re-played Blanton's memory of when he and his family purchased the cabin in South Africa, when he had told his wife he could not go for their most recent get-away, and how he had tucked the air ticket into the knapsack. He shot upward out of the tunnel soundlessly and left a gaping, perfectly round hole in the ceiling of the underground tunnel.

....

Meanwhile, Diamond and her family had returned home from a hectic day of shopping. They had eaten lunch and dinner, and the twins were already fast asleep. Jim was seated on the couch while watching a sports channel. Diamond was in the bedroom, fast asleep. She was too tired from the day's chores. She was dreaming.

Grey clouds covered the evening yellow sun. Diamond was standing right in front of her house, by the window to their living room. An ancient, worn-out ladder stretched from the ground to the heavens. Her eyes followed the ladder to see if she could estimate its height. Some of the steps of the ladder were broken, and some split from the middle. Others were completely missing. She had a strong urge to climb the ladder. She took the first step, then another, then a third, fourth, and fifth. The next three steps were missing. She noticed that the ladder got wider, further up. She looked around and towards the ground. The air was calm, but the ladder looked so battered that she strongly felt she would surely fall. Diamond re-traced her steps.

She woke up. The room was dark. She felt around for Jim on the bed. He was not beside her. She felt around for the light switch of the bedside table lamp and found it. She switched on the light and looked at the wall clock. It was 2:00 am. She remembered the dream and quickly got up from the bed and ran to the living room. Jim was already asleep and was snoring quietly. The T.V. was on a sports channel, and it was loud. Diamond grabbed the remote and turned down the volume of the T.V. Her eyes went to the window she saw in her dream. Approaching reluctantly but calmly, she drew back the window blind and peeped outside. Swaying slowly from side to side in the gentle night breeze was a silvery, worn-out-looking ladder. Diamond gasped and stepped back, frightened.

"This can't be," she whispered and looked at Jim. He was fast asleep. She took three deep breaths and drew back the curtain blind again. It was still there, swaying in the breeze with nothing supporting its weight as it reached the sky. Diamond screamed and fainted—an unfamiliar code displayed on the T.V.'s screen. The listening device was activated, sending coordinates to PIT with a message.

Ladder revealed at Lat 9.0878002 degrees. Lon 7.456380 Elev 487 meters.

Dracon was in the halo room when his watch began to flash red. He tapped on the watch's screen, and an incoming message icon was displayed. Dracon gasped and exclaimed loudly, "NO!" This was getting worse than he had anticipated. "But alas, this must mean that the one is at the same coordinate," he thought aloud.

Within a fraction of a second, he materialized in the halo room and focused on the coordinates.

All over the world, where it was daylight, people could see the sun surrounded by a rainbow. It was indeed beautiful to see the sight and the clicking sounds of snapshots followed by all sorts of cameras.

Jim jumped up from his sleep, awakened by Diamond's scream. She was falling towards the couch where he lay down. With quick reflexes he didn't know he had, he cushioned her fall in his arms and laid her gently on the sofa. She was murmuring, and he could hardly hear her. Just then, the power went off, and there was no light in the city. A common occurrence in Nigeria. The listening device on the T.V. automatically went off with the power.

Dracon had increased the intensity of the halo's penetrating ray.

Without warning, a cloudy beam of light suddenly shot out of the clouds from the night sky. A suya man was selling roasted meat to a small group. Others were smoking in groups, while another group was gambling. They all stopped their respective activities and became focused on the slowly descending white beam of light. The listening devices on their watches, phones, radio, and other electronic devices quickly sent messages to PIT about human awareness of strange and revealing events. Dracon promptly shut down the halo. He could not continue his search. Desperate, he opened a portal and was soon on Earth at the exact location. He transformed into a young, tall African man and stood before a fenced building. The fence wall was no barrier to him as he could see right through it. The building had four flats. All occupants were fast asleep. He could not read the people's thoughts. PIT had been unsuccessful in accessing human thoughts but could only obtain memories. Unless they were on a seduction mission and through connection to a selected human via a serum, they could only predict based on observed human behavioral patterns. He could not see the ladder either.

"It must have changed location and only revealed itself to someone at the time he received the alert," he thought as he looked around him. Everyone was talking about the beam of light that came from the sky.

"It was unbelievable, right?" Dracon asked the group closest to him.

He had turned away from the fenced building and mingled with the surprised crowd. Most ran into their makeshift shelters, built of straw and wood. Others stood boldly outside, talking about the event. Some had resumed their drinking and gambling.

When no one answered, Dracon tried another approach. "Maybe the world is coming to an end. How about the old ladder that appeared out of the sky? That was really frightening," he said in a loud voice so that others could hear him.

"Ladder! Kawaii! This man must be drunk!" someone from the small group said in Hausa. They all laughed and jeered at the strange-looking man.

"That means only the one must have seen the ladder," Dracon thought and continued his search.

"No wonder he is wearing a woman's shirt," another commented.

With a slight grin, Dracon walked away from the crowd, too immersed in his mission to find the one.

"What was he missing?" he asked as he stood at the very spot the ladder had appeared, just inside the fenced compound. The occupants were all still fast asleep.

"Nothing extraordinary about the couple and the kids in this flat," he thought as he increased his vibrational frequency and became invisible. This also enabled him to see the souls of the occupants. The woman was exceptionally bright. More than souls he had ever encountered. He connected to the Mainframe in PIT and ran a check. The Mainframe reads.

6365. Of the children of Seth. Known as Diamond Adeniyi on Earth. Working mother of two and a biochemist. Not popular with no significant achievement. No criminal records and no special interest. Happily married.

He paused the incoming message and materialized close to the woman's bed.

Jim lay beside his wife and was already fast asleep. Diamond was dreaming. When the halo was adjusted to focus on a certain coordinate, she saw an entity materialize in her bedroom.

Dracon tried to touch her. A substantial, thick, impenetrable wall of white light surrounded her. He looked at her sternly.

"In PIT, they had always succeeded in deeming any white light. It's been 2000 years since anyone had this type of light. It had always been so easy with humans, and this one should prove no different," thought Dracon as he stared at her.

She knew what the entity was thinking. Her body subconsciously flinched, trying to escape the entity's touch. Dracon was in awe.

"Interesting," he said and left Earth.

On PIT, a new project had already commenced. Ten thousand listeners instantly activated two miles around anywhere 6365 was. Their job was to extinguish the light at all costs. Also, a distraction was set in place with the primary purpose of deactivating the light.

Diamond was still asleep. The entity was no longer by her side, and she was outside in an open field. She saw an uncountable number of naked military men in uniform. A commander was shouting orders.

"Kill and destroy".

The men had super strength and were nothing like ordinary men. One of them turned to her and said, "Keep all this hidden and tell no one, for we have all been activated to take your life."

She woke up with a gasp.

CHAPTER THREE

DISTRACTION

3

It had been three days since Sarah spoke with her husband. She wondered why he had refused to join them this time.

"Blanton has always been the quiet one," she thought. They had been married for 25 years, and she could not have asked for a better man.

She had left Hog Hollow Country Lodge early that morning to call her husband at the restaurant 'That Place,' but no one picked up. Their family had made some rules for their getaway, which included no phone calls, no matter what. But she missed Blanton. This was the first time he'd missed camp.

The Buffels River passed right in front of the reserve. It was a beautiful silvery river, curving snake-like in its flow, ten miles to the west, towards the elephant sanctuary.

The air was clean and fresh, nothing like Massachusetts. She took a deep breath and held the railing firmly.

Someone covered her eyes from behind and whispered. "Guess who?".

She recognized the deep baritone voice and swirled around with joy.

"Sweetheart, I don't believe you are here. I called earlier this morning."

"Yes. I'm here. How are you and the kids?"

"We are fine," she answered, mimicking the voice of a robot as she tried to sound like him and laughed. "You sound so weird, love. What's up?" she asked.

The Listener looked into her eyes. They were teary and emotional.

"Just a bit tired from jet lag and, of course, work. I need to rest a while."

"Okay love. Would you like to eat something first?"

"Nope. I'm already full of all that airplane food."

"That's surprising! This will be the first time you'll be

turning down a South African delicacy," she said to him as she tried to ease out of his firm embrace. "He is acting like a robot," thought Sarah.

She watched him go towards the bedroom without asking where the kids were and followed him.

"Wow! Strange. Really strange," thought Sarah, who watched her husband fall asleep immediately after he hit the soft bed. "Not even a kiss," she said, murmuring. "He must be "fatigued. She turned around and padded out of the room.

"Hello, mom. Why are you sneaking out of the bedroom?" Blanton's son, Matthew, asked. He was with his sister.

"Dad is here...," she responded.

The kids were visibly excited and were about to burst into the room

"...and asleep," she said, silencing them back. "He is exhausted. Jet lag and all."

"Oh! Okay," they both responded. "So, how are the elephants," she asked.

"Great!" answered Jenny. We made some new friends too.

"Cool," Sarah responded.

"You don't seem excited mom. What's up?" asked Jenny as she flung her body onto the sofa on the balcony and picked a cookie from the table opposite the chair.

"Nothing much. Dad seems a bit weird," Sarah said, pausing for about six seconds as if looking for the right words. "Like a robot."

"Maybe Dad is a robot and is about to expire," Matthew said, starting to walk like a robot. "Maybe we are all robots, but we can only discover ourselves after forty."

Jenny threw a pebble at him and said, "No! Maybe we are cyborgs on a special mission."

Matthew caught the pebble and laughed, spilling some crumbs of cookies from his mouth.

"Alright, kids. No more robot talk. You guys are beginning to freak me out," said their mom amidst laughter.

"Sorry, Mom," said Jenny, biting on the last cookie from the now-empty bowl on the table.

"Yeah, mom. We are sorry. Do you know if Dad brought the catadioptric?"

"Not really. We didn't talk about that," replied his mom.

"I'll just check then," said Matthew as he started to walk quietly towards the door to his parent's room.

Sarah smiled as she watched the boy. He was the replica of his dad—very athletic and handsome. She wondered what girls must go through, knowing her son is reserved and does not believe in flirting. Maybe he has yet to meet a girl he adores. She wondered about the features of the yet-to-be-chosen girl and smiled. "She must be some angel," she said aloud.

"What did you say, Mom?" asked Jenny.

"Oh! Did I say that aloud? I must have been thinking aloud," replied Sarah.

"Matthew!" she called to her son, just as he was about to turn the handle of the bedroom door. "Please, bring me the nature magazine by the bedside table. Thanks. And try to be quiet".

He gave her a thumbs-up.

Jenny was scrolling through the pictures she had snapped of the elephant's coven and was smiling.

"Meet someone?" Sarah asked coyly.

"Just some new kids in SA for the first time.

From Israel," Jenny responded.

"Oh! Israel? Cool."

"We promised to show them some interesting sites tomorrow," said Jenny

"Cool. That'll give me and your dad some time alone together."

"Yeah! But what do old couples do when they're alone together, Mom? It's not like you guys are in your early forties!" Jenny asked, grinning.

"Hahaha," her mom said, jeering back.

"I wonder what's taking Matthew so long?" Sarah asked. Matthew was already in the room and staring at the man on the bed, perplexed.

"This man has my dad's face quite alright, but his demeanor was totally different. He seemed to be in a coma rather than asleep, and his color looked ashen. Maybe he is tired," thought Matthew.

He looked around the room for the

telescope. "Nothing," he whispered.

When he saw the knapsack beside the magazines on the bedside table and wanted to open it, he changed his mind and picked up a nature magazine instead.

"Hello, boy! Sneaking up on your dad?" his dad's voice froze him on the spot, just as he was about to open the door leading out of the room.

Matthew slowly turned to face the man. His dad's face looked bright, like his old dad. The boy sighed in relief.

"Dad!"

"Hey!" the Listener said as he got up from the bed in a swift move. "I was so worn out by the flight that I fell asleep immediately."

"No problem, Dad. Glad you could make it"

"Yeah. Me too," the Listener said and patted him on the shoulder.

"Okay!" Matthew exclaimed, dropping his hands from the hug he thought his dad wanted to give him and massaging his now-hurting shoulders. "I can see that you have been building up, Dad."

The Listener laughed and said, "Guess I don't know my own strength."

"Hey, guys?" Sarah called at the men. "Can see you are now awake. MATTHEW?

"I was very quiet, mum. Seriously," said Matthew defensively.

"Yes, he was," the Listener responded. "He didn't wake me up."

She walked to her husband's side and gave him a peck. "I've booked us dinner at The Place for 7:00 pm. You seem cold, love. Did you catch the flu?"

"Nope. I'm great. Just famished. Hey Matthew! I brought the telescope. Tonight is our night. After dinner. Okay?"

"Yippee! Sure, Dad," Matthew answered.

"I'm looking forward to it. I'll let you two be alone now," he said in a naughty tone and re-traced his steps backward, out of the room.

....

Back at Blanton's destroyed home, the dead man lay on the tunnel floor covered in debris. The police had already declared his house as an off-limits zone. The yellow tape surrounded what was remaining of the once beautiful apartment. Igdaleah knelt beside the body and examined him. He touched his broken neck, and it instantaneously healed. Blanton began to stir. Igdaleah disappeared.

At first, he could see only darkness. His throat felt stiff as if he had just recovered from choking. The image of being lifted off the ground and strangled flooded his memory. He wondered how he had survived. His vision had finally cleared.

Dim light from the evening sun streamed into the tunnel through the perfectly circular hole made by the Listener. Blanton looked around for his knapsack. He found his torch and staggered back through where he had come from. He climbed up the seared metallic steps into the basement. The apartment was unrecognizable. Nothing remained. No policemen or FBI were in sight. Even though it was nighttime and dark, he could still make out the yellow off-limit tape that sealed off the place. Suddenly light-headed from the shock of it all, he slumped to the floor and sat down heavily. Then he had a vision.

He saw himself and Matthew hiking on the Tsitsikamma mountain range. They got to a plateau and stopped. He brought out his telescope and set the mount on the rock. Matthew helped.

The vision stopped. Blanton was immediately alert. He shook his head to be sure he was alive.

"My brain must be scrambled," he thought as he looked around again. He raised his hoody above his head and walked into the dark, silent street. A policeman, parked in front of his neighbor's front porch, was too immersed in his hamburger to notice him. Blanton crossed the empty road to the 'Lumiere', a restaurant by the roadside. He was hungry. The aroma of the familiar Prime Hanger steak greeted his nostrils. As he approached the door, he rummaged through his pockets and found two crumpled $100 bills. The aroma of the steak was so strong that his mouth salivated as he sat down. A brunette approached him to take his orders. Blanton knew what he wanted already and did not bother going through the menu. He gave his order, and she wrote it down. The sound from the siren of a police vehicle on patrol startled him as the brunette tried to confirm his orders.

"Prime hanger steaks and a side dish of sautéed drumlin farm greens, chili flakes, and garlic butter, Sir?"

"Yes. Thank you," answered Blanton. "I shouldn't be here," he thought.

The LCD TV on the wall was emitting a low-toned sound of the 8:00 p.m. news. A young couple was seated adjacent to him, and they reminded him of Sarah. A flash of the previous vision filled his mind, and he felt light-headed again and had another vision.

He was in bed with Sarah at the Hog Hollow Country Lodge. Sarah was fast asleep, and a beam of light shot out from both his eyes, directed at her forehead, scanning her brain.

"Here's your order, Sir," the brunette said. Her voice snapped him back to reality. She looked at him queerly and asked, "You sure you're alright Sir?" in a heavy Scandinavian accent.

"Yes! I'm fine. Can I have a glass of water?" She walked away to do his bidding. Blanton could not eat. His thoughts were on a rampage. "Why this visions of him in South Africa with his family? He did not get a good look at the entity that strangled him. "Definitely from PIT. Did the thing take my knapsack? Oh goodness!" He remembered his flight ticket. He felt light-headed again and had another vision.

He was standing by the window as if looking at the stars. Sarah was fast asleep. He keyed in some codes into his digital watch and a hologram appeared. It was Band, the Lord of War.

"Awaiting your orders, Sir. The man's family knows nothing about 7632's findings," the Listener said to the hologram.

"Great! Get rid of them. But not now. Do it in 72 hours. We need a body to make it seem he died in SA. You have not boarded a flight, and that's an issue. We need people to think he traveled for vacation. Make it look like an accident."

The hologram dissipated.

Blanton became frantic as the vision stopped. He had only three days to save his family, but what could he do? Walking rapidly to the same waitress and trying to look composed, he asked, "I need your help. I need to reschedule my flight. I had made a mental note to reschedule but totally got distracted and forgot."

She raised an eyebrow. Wondering what he was talking about.

"Do you have a computer with internet that I can use?" he asked.

"Sure. Just down the hallway on your left. It's on the house. It's part of our value-added service. So, it's no problem."

"Thank you so much," he said and dashed towards the direction she pointed and was soon surfing the net. He booked an 11:00 pm flight to SA.

He heard someone in the restaurant ask that the volume of the T.V be increased. The news headline read.

Mystery explosion at top scientist apartment.

Blanton's face was displayed on the screen. Blanton dashed for the exit door. The brunette called at him and stopped him in his tracks.

"Sir!"

His heart began to beat fast. He waited for the confirmation that she recognized him.

"I hope you enjoyed your meal and will come back again."

"Yes. Yes. Thank you," he stammered without turning to face her, walking into the cold night. With his hand dipped into his right pocket, he checked if he had change left. $150. That should do. A quick wave at the oncoming taxi, and a yellow cab screeched to a halt before him.

"Airport real fast," commanded the scientist.

"Yes sir," the cab driver replied in an Indian accent as Blanton closed the taxi door.

....

At the Nnamdi Azikiwe International Airport, Diamond hugged her family. She had been invited to present on her successful research project in South Africa for two weeks.

"It was a welcomed distraction. At least I can escape for a while from my house. Maybe the dreams will stop now," she thought, kissing her kids' forehead and giving Jim a warm hug.

"I'll miss you guys," she said.

"We'll miss you too," Jim responded.

"Mom?"

"Yes, love."

"Buy me a South African Superman," the young boy said, pulling at her sleeve to get attention.

Everyone laughed.

"Why do you need a South African Superman? Superman is the same everywhere." Daisy said harshly.

"No! I want a South African Superman mommy." "Don't argue, guys. I'll look for a South African Superman love..."

"Thanks, mom," said David

"...and a South African Supergirl," their mum said, with her eyes focused on Daisy with a wink."

"Ah! There is nothing like a South African Supergirl mommy. That is totally impossible!" the little girl exclaimed with her palms pressing both sides of her cheeks and her eyeballs wide open. "But I won't mind if you find one."

Diamond laughed. When she heard the flight announcement, she quickly gave more kisses and rushed off, waving to her family again.

"That woman has a lot on her mind," Jim thought as he waved back at his beautiful wife. "But she has been so stubborn not to say anything." He looked at her as she walked out of sight. He loved her model figure. She did not look anything like a mother of two. Neither did she look like she had been having disturbing dreams. "Maybe they are not that serious." But he was still worried. He had always known her as a very deep woman, with strange ideas, such that the most used search engine in the world does not have an answer to some of her questions. Also, it was brilliant. He would wait patiently until she was ready to share what troubled her with him.

"Daddy? Is that mom's flight?" David asked as a plane flew overhead.

"Maybe," answered Jim.

"That means she can see us from the window," said David

"Maybe," answered Jim

"Dad, we want a yes or no and not maybe," Daisy said.

"Okay. Yes," answered Jim.

"Yippee. Let's wave at Mommy Daisy," said David.

"Or, no," said their dad as they were about to wave.

"Oh! Dad," they both said in frustration, swinging their tiny hands above their heads.

"Okay. I'll make a deal with you guys. If you are good, I'll buy you something special each day your mom is gone," their dad offered.

"Can we have a secret meeting, Daisy?" David asked as he pulled her to the side. They went some distance from Jim's side and whispered in each other's ears.

"Hmm! A secret plan, sheesh!" said Jim, his hands in akimbo and his left foot tapping softly on the marble floor.

Another dad was standing nearby with his kids and laughed. "Kids are so funny," he said.

"Most certainly, sir," Jim responded and smiled.

"My wife also just went on a trip to a conference in S.A," the man continued.

"Oh! Maybe she'll meet my wife," She's also traveling for a conference at S.A.

"That's cool. Small world right," said the man. "Yeah!" Jim responded

"Okay, Dad. We have decided. We get to choose what we want, "said the twins in unison, interrupting their dad's discussion with the stranger.

"How about we go and have ice cream first, then we'll talk," said Jim.

"Cool," they both echoed.

Jim waved at the man as the twins pulled him towards the direction of the ice cream stand they knew only too well.

Sed looked at Jim severely as he turned a corner with his children and was soon out of his view. He had scanned Jim's brain the whole time they had the short conversation. His kids were no longer in sight. They had been holograms. Nothing in Jim's memory revealed any information whatsoever about PIT.

"Maybe the woman does not know anything about PIT, and Dracon was only getting worked up," the man thought.

"Even if she had the brightest flame of white light, none has been able to retain the brilliance for long. It won't be a difficult task at all," thought Sed.

"We are sorry for the delay in the departure flight of ADK 005A from Abuja Nnamdi Azikiwe Airport to Cape Town International, South Africa. We anticipate take-off in 30 minutes," boomed a female voice over the airport speakers.

Sed smiled. He had caused the pilot to report a 30 minutes' delay. He walked into the boarding area confidently.

"Such a clueless and fascinating race," he said and walked towards the boarding area.

Diamond could not wait to be airborne. A tall lanky man walked towards her direction, searching for his seat number. The man had blonde hair and sky-blue eyes. She had seen and met lots of handsome men, but this man's physical features and persona were beyond perfect.

"Wow!" she thought. "God really took time in molding this one."

Sed caught her staring at him. He was not surprised. He got that a lot. He pressed a button on his ring. A colorless liquid oozed out onto his right palm. He smiled and said, "Excuse me, lady".

"Oh, sorry!" she said and moved so he could cross over to the window seat.

"Hi! I'm Sed," he said and smiled, stretching his hand for a handshake.

"I'm Diamond," she responded and shook his hand. It felt strangely very warm and comforting.

He looked deep into her eyes and held her palm for seconds longer.

She felt slightly light-headed. He finally let go, and she was pleased he did, but her throat felt dry.

"Okay. Very good-looking man. But that should not concern me. I'm happily married," thought Diamond. Her hand still felt tingly and warm from the shake, and she wondered why.

"Is this your first time?" Sed asked, trying to strike up a conversation with the woman.

"First time for what?" she asked. "first time to meet a really handsome dude? Yeah!" she thought.

"First time traveling through air," he said.

"Nope," she responded.

"Cool. I'm attending a conference in SA,"

said Sed. She did not utter a word in response.

"I'm participating in this conference because of the presentation from a superb biochemist. She'll be speaking on a discovery. A true panacea that can cure all forms of cancer," said Sed, not deterred.

Diamond smiled and said, "Okay, that sounds interesting," she pretended it was not her.

He brought the conference bulletin and began to read it as the plane took off into the clear blue sky.

Sed sensed that the serum from his ring was beginning to take effect as Diamond touched her cheek with the palm she shook his hand with. It was supposed to heighten her testosterone and create in her mind an impression of him, such that he would always be in her thoughts.

The tingling had reduced, and her palm felt

less warm. She checked her digital wristwatch.

"Two hours of flight already. Wow! How time flies," she thought. Her mind returned to her family, and she smiled, remembering David's request for an African Superman. The strong desire to be with her family suddenly overwhelmed her. Two weeks away won't be as easy as she had thought. Her mind wandered to her dreams, but she shrugged off the thoughts. The voice of the air hostess interrupted her thoughts.

"Would you like water, a beverage, or wine?"

"I'll have water. Thank you," said Diamond.

"Water for me also," said Sed.

The hostess passed a sealed plastic water bottle to Diamond and another to Sed.

"Would you prefer chicken or beef meals?" the hostess asked.

In her service cart were wrapped meals of

rice and salad with either chicken or beef sauce. Each wrap also had beverage and sugar in sachets, pasteurized milk in a small jug, and a dessert of ice cream sundaes.

"I'll have chicken. Thank you," said Diamond.

"I'll have Chicken also. Thank you," said Sed.

"Here you go," said the hostess as she passed them the wrapped meals and pushed on the trolley to serve the passengers in front.

Diamond did not realize how hungry she was and quickly dived into the meal.

"Hmm! Nice," commented Sed after tasting the chicken sauce.

"And fresh," added Diamond.

"Yeah, it's much better than last time. Nigerians are not used to eating like this, right?" Sed asked.

"What do you mean?" asked Diamond, who had already started eating her dessert.

Sed smiled and said, "A question for a question. That's a Nigerian thing."

Diamond smiled but said nothing.

"You guys serve one meal. For instance, you could have Moi-Moi and your local cereal 'pap' as breakfast, then pounded yam and egusi soup as lunch. Nothing like a three-course meal during each meal time," explained Sed.

"Wow! Seems you've been in Naija for quite some time," responded Diamond.

"Yeah. For some years now. I like the way you said Naija. Sounds sweet. Nothing like the way it usually sounds with other Nigerians I have been in conversation with," said Sed.

"Really? How did the other Nigerians sound?" asked Diamond.

"Naija!" exclaimed Sed, trying to mimic the

Nigerian accent.

Diamond laughed as she put aside her empty meal pack, throwing her head back as she did so. Her long waist-length, tightly coiled kinks escaped from the bun that was loosely holding the strands in place. The coils from the twist-out style now framed her face.

"I can't believe you just said that," she said amidst laughter and tucked the strands covering her face behind her ears; her eyes were misty.

Sed looked at the waist-length kinky coils.

"You've got adorable hair. It's difficult to see a West African woman with really long kinks like yours."

Diamond wiped her tear-filled eyes with a green check-designed handkerchief and said, "There are quite a number of West African women with long hair. Most of them cover it up."

"You married?" Sed asked.

"Yes, with two kids. Twins."

"Naaa! That's not true. You don't look it."

"Thanks. I'll take that as a compliment. And you? Are you married?"

"Not yet. I'm confident you'd be the one if I had met you before you married.

Diamond laughed again and said. "That's nice. I think you like to flatter people. Anyway, I love flattery. My husband does that too."

Sed smiled. "This is going well," he thought.

....

Blanton was already in mid-air and worried about how he would face the imposter who was with his family.

"That is if the visions are true. We are in real trouble if it's the same entity that attacked me. How will I fight or even subdue something with unbelievable strength?" he thought.

The memory of his death experience filled his mind. He shuddered. He stared at the untouched meal pack on the tray table before him. It was already cold, and he did not feel hungry. His mind wandered over the event that started this uncertain journey in his life. He desperately wished that he did not know what he now knew.

"How would he find this person that would help the Earth? What does he look like? Where is he? Why wasn't he told who it was and how to reach him," Blanton thought, feeling so much despair.

The flight attendant passed by his seat with the service cart and collected the untouched meal pack. She smiled at Blanton and asked, "I hope you are doing fine, Sir?"

"I'm great. Thanks. Just seem to have lost my appetite."

"That's fine, Sir."

Twenty minutes later, the captain announced the descent and final approach to their destination.

"Ladies and gentlemen, as we start our descent, please ensure your tray tables are in full upright positions. Ensure your seatbelt is securely fastened and all carry-on luggage is stowed underneath the seat in front of you or the overhead bins. Thank you."

Blanton's heartbeat suddenly increased when he heard they were already in S.A. and approaching the airport. He remembered the giant that squeezed the life out of him.

"If only Igdaleah were here," he thought.

He felt sure he would recognize 'the one' when he saw him.' He also felt strongly that he would overcome the imposter, but how all this would happen eluded him.

As the airplane flew onto the runway, Blanton felt the airspeed reduce. The pilot kept the airspeed well above stall speed and at a constant rate of descent. At touch down, Blanton closed his eyes and took a deep breath.

"I'm ready," he mumbled.

Blanton walked through the arrivals section on the lower floor of the airport building. His feet were soundless on the marble floor. A shoulder gently brushed his side and startled him. He looked at the lady, who smiled and winked at him. He smiled back and walked on. Each step brought him closer to his destination, and he felt weary. He walked further from the airport to the highway, deciding not to take one of the readily available airport shuttles. He decided to board the town's local minibus, too troubled to engage one of the registered airport shuttles. This would give him time to plan; it was his first time boarding a minibus, and he did not care about theft. There were bigger problems ahead of him than a minor theft.

Blanton waved down an approaching minibus. Luckily, this one was not full, and the driver pulled off the highway to the bus station, where Blanton was waiting.

"Hog Hollow?" asked Blanton.

"Enter," said the conductor as he moved out of Blanton's way so that he could enter.

South African music blared in the bus—almost deafening. He was the only non-African on the crowded bus and was lucky to get one going directly to Hog Hollow.

"Jou tarief", the conductor said to Blanton.

"Hoeveel?" replied Blanton

"50 rand", answered the conductor.

"Jy nem dollars? Ek het net dollars",

Blanton told the conductor he only had dollars.

"Goed. Gee, my 5 dollars." the conductor responded.

Blanton rummaged through his pocket and gave him 10 dollars.

The man gave Blanton 70 rand as change.

He did not care that he had been cheated.

....

Diamond had slept during the final two hours before landing. She decided to spend the night at the airport lodge, hoping to rest a day, before proceeding to the conference venue at Antler's Lodge. Sed, on the other hand, had already proceeded to the conference venue. Diamond was glad she did not have to ride with him on the five-hour, 43-minute journey. She already had enough of the tingling in her stomach while sitting beside him in the airplane. He made her feel uncomfortable and flirty.

"These feelings are not welcome," she thought, forcing her mind to think of Jim, but it kept returning to Sed.

Sed was also worn out from the drive to Antler's Lodge. Being on Earth can be tiresome to the Pitalunans. The oxygen level on PIT was one-third of that on Earth. He looked at his surroundings with disgust. "Too much nature here," he thought.

His cabin was set away from the rest of the Lodge. It had a private luxury room, tastefully decorated in African style, and was more expensive than the others. He knew that Diamond's cabin was just next door and anxiously awaited her arrival. He liked the woman, which was rather unusual. Though the Pitalunans were jealous of the light around humans and would do anything within their power to either dim or totally extinguish it, they were equally attracted to it. This was because they were once light beings before the fall.

"I don't think the serum is taking as much effect as it should. I'll probably increase the dosage next time. After her speech, though. Don't want to have a horny woman upstage in front of all those people," Sed thought and smiled curiously as he threw himself on the neatly laid bamboo bed, covered with a soft mattress and deep purple comforter. He was soon fast asleep.

Diamond woke up early the next day. She had checked out early and was outside, waiting for her hired cab. She looked at her watch. The Casio stainless steel watch read 90C and 7:00 am. The conference starts tomorrow, and she will have enough time to prepare. The sound of a car's horn interrupted her thoughts. She looked up. A white cab pulled over to her side. The driver got out and walked towards her.

"Good morning, Madam. Are you Mrs. Jim? he asked.

"Yes. I am," she replied.

"I am Timothy, the driver you called," he said, showing her his ID.

"Great! Thanks for arriving early," she said and pointed to her luggage.

She had been standing for only one minute when she noticed a man dressed in a hood standing about six feet away.

"Cold morning, hey?" the driver said, with a thick accent, as he opened the car door for her to enter.

"Yes. It is rather cold," Diamond responded, holding her arms around her body as she entered the car.

"We will be going on a 5-hour journey. Would you like to pick up something to eat on the way?" the driver asked.

"Hmm. Not re...."

Diamond was still talking when the face of the man with the hood appeared by her window.

"Ahh!" she screamed, startled by the sudden appearance of his face, pressed to her window.

"So sorry to startle you, ma'am," the man said, as the driver rushed over to her side and pushed at the stranger, while at the same time alerting the security.

A security man approached the group and brought out his taser.

"I don't want any trouble. Ek wil enigie problem," the hooded stranger said, repeating his words in Afrikaans. "Something dropped from the lady's purse, and I wanted to give it to her."

The security man paused. Diamond checked her bag. It was not open.

She shrugged and rolled down her window to collect a pen from the outstretched hand.

"Thank you," she said uncertainly and rolled up the glass.

"You are most welcome," said the stranger. He bowed and left.

The security man returned his taser to its pouch and said, "Keep safe, madam, and enjoy South Africa." He turned around sharply and returned to his post.

Diamond waved at him and smiled.

The cab driver sped off. She did not see the cab driver wink back at the hooded man.

She began to feel slightly dizzy and thought it must be from the fright the stranger gave her.

Within 20 minutes, Diamond was knocked unconscious from the drug-laced in the pen.

....

Blanton stood some meters away from Hog Hollow Country Lodge, hidden from sight by the trees of the Kynsna Amatole Montane forest. A gentle sea breeze blew through the vibrant upscale Lodge and rustled the leaves of the White and Red Alder trees that surrounded him. He could see his family having breakfast on the front pouch. Their cabin was secluded from other apartments by a group of surrounding trees. In front of it was an open carpet grass field about 5 meters wide. He inched closer to get a better view. He was seated, right there, with his family, watching them closely.

"How can this be? What was the entity that took his form, and why was it with his family?"

A deep baritone laughter echoed from the small group. It sounded just like his. Blanton was alarmed.

"What am I going to do? The imposter sounds just like me," thought Blanton.

He saw Sarah lean over to kiss his clone. Blanton became very angry.

"How was he going to defeat an alien who moved faster than the speed of light?" thought Blanton.

Meanwhile, in Antler's Lodge, Sed got impatient waiting for Diamond. The serum injected into her palm during the handshake also enabled him to track her. Though it was not permanent and would only last for two weeks, this was more than enough time to complete his task. Sed remembered his most extended task. It lasted only two days; he had already spent 48 hours on this task and had yet to achieve much. His mind went back to Diamond. He looked at his watch.

"She should be here in 2 hours," he thought.

He activated his tracking device and received the coordinates of her location. He focused the lens on Diamond's coordinates through remote access to the satellite. His watch's screen glimmered, and the image of the unconscious woman was on the screen. Sed scanned for her vitals. The screen displayed the readings.

"Heartbeat, normal. Presence of basfulage detected in the bloodstream."

Sed increased the focus area. A man was driving. He also struggled to focus on the road while talking through his mobile phone, which was held in place and pressed to his ear between his left shoulder and left cheek.

"Ja. Sal lewer the pakkie in ongeveer 2 uur," the cab driver said in a deep Afrikaans ascent.

"Speak English, man," commanded the voice at the end of the line.

"I said the parcel should arrive in about 2 hours," said the driver.

"That's not good at all. The sleep drug would have worn off by then. Where exactly are you now?" the voice asked.

"We are on Settlers Way/N2," the driver responded. "Good. That's a very lonely place. Just park close to the woods and give her another dose. I hope you have the syringe," the voice asked.

"Yes. I have it," said the driver.

"She will make a perfect ransom. Just hurry and get here quickly," the voice said, and the call was dropped.

The cab driver allowed the phone to fall off his shoulder onto his lap.

"Crazy man," the driver murmured as he drove off road N2 into the nearby group of trees.

Without waiting for a second longer, Sed initiated the transporter on his watch. He began to de-atomize and fade.

The driver had found the perfect spot. Diamond was already becoming conscious. She was moving slightly and grunting as if in pain. She tried opening her eyes, but everything was hazy. Her head hurt so badly. She heard a man's voice say,

"Don't worry, sleeping beauty; you will soon be back to sleep and continue the lovely dreams. Okay"

"Back to sleep? Why did he want her back to sleep? she wondered.

Her vision was becoming clearer, and so was her memory. She remembered she was on her way to Antler's Lodge, then became dizzy. She remembered the odor from the pen the hooded man gave her. She became afraid and tried to speak.

"Shh! Don't worry, this won't hurt at all," the driver said.

Diamond became frantic and tried to move,

but felt paralyzed. The driver heard a sparking-static sound in the woods. He turned towards the direction of the sound. The faded outline of a man appeared to his right. He saw the head materialize, then other parts of the body.

"HERE GOD!" the driver exclaimed in his dialect. Diamond heard the sound, too, but could not turn her head towards it. Sed had materialized at Diamond's coordinates. He had adjusted to 2 meters away from the exact spot so that he would not merge into her body on re-atomizing. The driver could not move. The syringe had dropped from his shaking hands, and his trousers were wet. Sed looked at Diamond and scanned her Vitals. The driver saw a red beam of light coming from the man's eyes, and his strength suddenly returned to him. He took to his heels.

"She is fine. You are lucky you did not hurt

her," Sed said to the running man.

He pressed a button on his watch, and a giant energy beam shaped like a hand went forth and lifted the man into space. A short scream and silence followed. The driver lay, looking lifeless on the beam's palms. A white beam from Sed's eyes took away his memory of the encounter but left it just at the point where he was about to inject the helpless woman. The energy beam laid him on the ground under one of the trees.

Diamond was beginning to regain her strength and could move her upper torso. She turned her head towards the sounds.

"Sed!" she called, surprised and even more confused.

"You'll be alright now," said Sed.

He went quickly to her side and lifted her off the ground. She felt light in his arms. He could read absolutely everything that was happening within her body.

"The curse of the Pitalunans," Sed thought as he placed her on the back seat.

Diamond felt dizzy again. Her mind could not process what had happened, so she drifted off. Sed sat in the driver's seat. He looked back at Diamond. She was asleep.

"Good, " he said, driving down the remaining stretch of road N2 towards Antler's Lodge.

....

The scientist needed a plan. He knew he could not risk walking through the open field toward the cabin. That would be signing his death warrant again. He grimaced as the image of being strangled flooded his mind. His family had vacated at Hogs Hollow severally, and he knew the Lodge like the back of his hand. A thicket of wood was behind their cabin. He walked further into the woods and climbed the tallest tree he could find. It was high enough to give him a view of what was happening and carve out his plan. His family had just finished breakfast and were playing a game of throw-ball in the open field. His cabin was surrounded by dense wood with three inlets from the Northeast direction, but only one inlet from Northwest. He had to set a trap. There were lots of bamboo trees around the area.

"Bamboos provide good string," Blanton said and set to work.

He climbed down the tree and pulled at one of the thick vines on his way down. He tied the vines around a thicket of tall bamboo trees at their base. He gathered more vines and tied them around severally onto the middle and up to the top until he had a single, firm, closely knitted bunch of bamboo. He gathered more vines and passed them together, through the tied bamboo, onto the top of a strong branch on a pear tree, and jumped down towards the ground from the tree. His weight pulled the tree's top towards the Earth until it almost touched the ground. He drew the vines around a massive rock. The spring of the bamboo prevented the thick set of vines from snapping. He then extended the remaining length of the vines, placed low to the ground, and tied to an opposite tree, just a foot away. He hoped his estimate would be correct since he did not have his measuring tape. Looking at his trap again, he set out towards the cabin through the Northwest entrance.

Meanwhile, Sed had reached Antlers Lodge and carried Diamond into his cabin. He felt a strange warmth in his heart. An old memory came to his mind. It was a time when all he had ever felt was love, and everything was perfect.

"If only they had not rebelled," he thought, placing the sleeping woman on his bed. He looked at her once more and went out of the bedroom.

Not too far from Antlers Lodge, about 21.4 kilometers southwest in Orchids Valley, Blanton entered his cabin from the back door. His family was still outside with the imposter, playing the same game. He looked around for a clue. There was nothing. No objects that belong to the alien could be found to give him a clue. From his earlier vision, his family had 48 hours to live, and now, only 6 hours were left. He had to get the entity's attention without being detected by his wife or children.

Matthew became tired and thirsty from

throwing balls. He needed something chilled.

"Dad!" Matthew called, signaling a time-out with his hands.

The alien paused with the ball in his hands.

"I need a time-out, going in for a drink," said Matthew.

"Cool. No problem," replied the Listener.

The Listener scanned the boy and said, "The water will do you some good. Make sure it's not too chilled."

"Sure thing, Dad," responded Matthew as he walked towards the front door of their cabin.

Blanton was thinking of how he would get the Listener's attention when the front door swung open. Before him stood a shocked young man, staring as if he had seen a ghost and looking utterly confused.

"Dad," Matthew said almost inaudibly. His voice was lost from the shock.

This man before him looked rough, with his beard all grown and unkempt. He had only seen his dad like this when he planned for the trip to Mars. The man was so excited and busy that he did not even have time to shave.

The scientist sprang into action and, in two leaps, was at the young man's side. He covered Matthew's mouth and dragged him down, away from the window.

"Shhh," Blanton said, his hands still over the boy's mouth.

The young man tried to get free. Blanton held him firmly with all his might.

"Matthew. Matthew. Listen to me."

Matthew struggled harder.

"You have to listen. The man out there is not me. I know you do not believe me. I also know we have promised not to switch on our phones here. But I will allow you to go to the main Lodge. Connect to the internet with your mobile and read the main news."

Matthew stopped struggling.

Blanton continued without reducing his hold. "Our house has been blown up. I came across some discovery that jeopardizes all of humanity and my family. We have 4 hours before that alien destroys us all. I know you don't believe me, but..."

The sound of approaching footsteps cut him short.

"I need you to go into the main Lodge now. I'll be in the woods at our secret spot. Don't tell anyone because this thing is too powerful even for the military," said Blanton as he released the confused boy and ran towards the back exit, whispering one more sentence at the door.

"Sing - the river is here - in your mind, and don't stop singing it until you meet me," whispered Blanton as he disappeared into the woods.

Matthew sat on the floor, dazed and processing what had just happened. The door opened, and a head peered in.

"Matthew!" his dad's voice called.

The boy was startled at the sound and looked at the caller.

His dad was dressed in khaki and jersey, with his beard trimmed.

"I heard a struggle. Are you alright?" the man asked.

"Yes. I'm fine," answered Matthew as he stood up, stammering. "I tripped on my foot and fell here," the young man said, pointing to the floor behind him.

"Well, you look fine. I'm also thirsty. You had your drink yet?" asked the alien.

"This man looks more like my dad than the rough one. But the rough one seems more human than this one," thought Matthew, not hearing the question from the man.

"Matthew?"

"I'm cool, Dad," he said aloud. "Or alien," he said in his mind.

"I'll just go to the main Lodge to get some coke. Do you want a coke?" asked Matthew.

"No. I'm good," said the Listener. He wondered why the boy was trying so hard to look relaxed.

Matthew had already turned away, and the Listener tried to scan his brain. All he heard was the song – the river is here.

....

Back in Sed's room, Diamond woke up startled. Her dream of the Earth falling into a deep, dark gorge frightened her. Her eyes were still closed. She felt around with her hands. It felt soft. She could smell coffee. She opened her eyes and wrinkled her nostrils. She does not like coffee. She was in the Antler's cabin. She knew from the bamboo walls and the strong, distinct smell of Red Alder trees that were peculiar to the place. Sitting upright and leaning her back against the head of the bed, she observed her surroundings.

"Was it all a bad dream?" she wondered.

An image of a man with a syringe flooded her memory, and she remembered everything.

"Sed," she said quietly.

"Was she in Sed's room?" she thought.

She suddenly became self-aware and checked if she was naked.

"Gosh! Only her shoes were off. Thank goodness."

Just then, Sed walked in.

Diamond pulled the blanket around her neck instinctively.

"I can see you are up. Good. How do you feel?" Sed asked the woman, ignoring her action with the blanket. She had drawn it further up to her chin.

"Good. Thank you," she said, looking at him quizzically. "How did you know where to find me?"

"I think you need to rest first," said Sed, passing her a cup of coffee.

She turned her face away from the steam. "Thanks, but I don't take coffee," she said.

She slid her legs off the bed onto the ground and tried to stand up. Sed was immediately by her side, holding her in a firm embrace to prevent an inevitable fall. She felt her stomach tingle.

"I'm okay," she said shyly and tried to pull herself away. He did not permit her. Instead, he looked deep into her coffee-brown eyes with their faces only inches apart.

"You are sure?" Sed asked. His voice had gone slightly faint from the emotions he felt after reading the worry in her eyes.

"Yes," answered Diamond with a shaky voice.

He let her go, propping her gently on the bed, and backed away two steps.

"But I'm hungry," she said quietly. "Hopefully, that would get him far away from this room," she thought.

Sed smiled. He felt wicked because her mind was like an open book to him, and he could read it at will. Because she was already connected to him, he had control due to the serum in her system.

"The serum!" he exclaimed in his mind. This may be the best time to give her another dose.

However, when he looked at her, Sed changed his mind. "When she is asleep, I will give her the dose," he thought.

"Okay. What would you like to eat?" he asked Diamond.

"I would love anything light you might have.

I need to regain my strength for tomorrow's conference."

"Yes, the conference; I think your health is much more important than that right now."

She did not respond but slowly slid under the covers.

"I'll get you something to eat," Sed said and left the room.

Diamond quickly removed the blanket and tried once more to stand. She almost fell but promptly held onto the bed. She let out a frustrated sigh.

"I have to walk. Need to get out of here before he gets back," she said and struggled until she could finally stand. She took a step and staggered a bit. Then, she took another and felt better. She walked over to where her shoes and jacket were, picked each up, and looked out the window. Sed had just entered the reception area.

She wore her shoes and jacket, picked up

her handbag that was on the table, and quietly slid out of the room through the back door that led directly outside.

On approaching the reception area, she saw Sed sitting in the guest lounge, apparently waiting for her food. She needed him out, so she could find out which cabin was hers and collect her room keys.

"I hope it's on the other side, far away from him," she thought.

A beautiful young lady approached Sed with a sealed tray of toast bread, scrambled eggs, and a Greek salad. On the side, there was a sealed can of Greek yogurt. She struck a seductive pose at the handsome man.

"Can I take this to your room, sir?"

"Oh! Is it ready? That was fast. Thanks. Not to worry," he said with a smile and collected the tray, anxious to return to his cabin. He was surprised to find himself already missing the woman.

Diamond saw him walking towards the door and quickly hid behind the flowers outside the building.

Sed passed by whistling. He paused briefly and sniffed the air. He thought he perceived Diamond. She had an intoxicating feminine aroma, which lacked any cologne. It was rare to meet an earthly woman who did not wear perfume or makeup. Diamond was exceptional, and he liked it. The aroma of fresh coconut lingered. He shrugged and walked on, thinking she must definitely still be in bed.

Diamond almost gasped. "Did he see her?" she thought but relaxed as he continued towards his cabin, whistling a non-familiar tune.

She quickly entered the reception area and engaged the receptionist. "Hello. I'm Mrs. Jim. I would like to check in."

"Good evening, madam. We have been expecting you. How was your flight?" the receptionist asked.

"Great! I am tired. Can you make this real quick? I don't mean to be rude, but I need to do some stuff. You know, female stuff," she explained, gesturing with her hands to signal what the sign of female stuff meant.

The receptionist, confused at first, finally said, "Oh, okay. I understand. Female stuff," and smiled. Here are your keys, madam. Your cabin is just down there. Not far away at all," the receptionist said, pointing to the cabin beside Seds.

"Oh, my goodness," Diamond exclaimed.

"Don't you like the cabin?" the receptionist asked worriedly.

"It's okay," Diamond responded. She could see that Sed was almost at his cabin door but stopped to speak with someone.

"It's fine. Don't you have another cabin

further into the estate?" inquired Diamond.

The receptionist scanned her records quickly, seeing that her guest seemed in a hurry.

"All rooms are fully booked," she said as nicely as possible.

"No problem," Diamond said over her shoulders, as she was already on her way out. She took another path so that Sed would not see her approaching.

She got to her cabin undetected and entered through the back door.

"Phew!" she exclaimed, letting out a deep sigh. She ran into the bedroom and flung herself onto the inviting soft bed.

"All alone at last. No Sed or some weird driver trying to kidnap me. No funny butterfly feelings and stuff," she said aloud, hugging a pillow and rolling around like a happy teenager.

A buzzing sound shook her handbag. She

looked at it curiously and then smiled after a moment.

"My phone. It must be Jim," she said, opening the bag to pick up the phone. She remembered their last conversation was just before she checked out of the airport hotel. It's been over 12 hours, and Jim had been worried about her.

"Hello," she said quietly into the phone.

"Hello. Seems you have forgotten all about us already," Jim said, sounding worried.

"So many things happened on the way, love. But I'm fine, and I cannot forget my loved ones," she said, feeling guilty as she remembered Sed.

Sed reached his cabin. A stranger had stopped him to say hello and engaged him in a conversation that was of no interest to him. All he wanted to do was be with the earthling who made him feel the way he had forgotten how to feel. After the fall, he had spent his life hurting and destroying relationships. Now, more anxious to see Diamond, he closed the door gently behind him and went straight to the bedroom. She was not there. He had to give her another shot of the seductive serum. But, now, he would prefer that she come to like him.

But what was he thinking? He had a job to do, and Dracon would not want to hear that he fell for an earthly woman.

"She must have felt better and decided to leave," thought Sed. He walked towards his bedroom window and peered through the glass at the nearby cabin. A woman's figure was walking back and forth in the living room. He smiled and walked towards the wardrobe. He opened it. Her luggage was still there. He carried the luggage and the tray of food and left for her cabin.

Diamond had just finished her call with Jim. She was restless and pacing around the living room the whole time they talked. Usually, she would have told Jim about the people she met and the incidents that occurred. They did not hide things from each other. But this was a whole new ball game. She felt something for the stranger. It was something she could not decipher.

"Why? Why? Why?" she asked repeatedly, throwing her hands in the air; then, a knock at the front door interrupted her thoughts.

"Sed!" said Diamond in a whisper. Her mouth involuntarily uttering the name. She stood frozen, contemplating whether to answer.

"Hello, Diamond," said Sed. His voice echoed into the cozy room. "I brought your luggage."

He paused a while, but still no answer. "You seem to be feeling well. I know you are in the living room. I can see you through the curtains."

Diamond immediately walked to the door and turned the knob gently but quickly. There he was in all his brilliance. The light from the room reflected into his blue eyes. It was so much light that he squinted them a little, which gave him an even more seductive gaze. He looked at her straight in the eyes and said with a smile, "You look well." His perfect white teeth were too much for her, and the thoughts popping up in her mind shocked her.

"I brought your luggage and, of course, your food," he said with a hint of sadness.

Diamond found her voice.

"Yes," she said, stammering. "Thank you so much." She stretched her hands to collect the luggage and the sealed food tray.

Sed passed her the food tray. "This one is too heavy for you," he said, carrying the luggage into the room and dropping the massive box on the wooden floor in the middle of the living room. "You don't need to carry heavy stuff yet," he said, turning around to face her.

Sed's presence shook Diamond. She felt light-headed and did not observe that he was standing too close by. She could hardly control her emotions for this man. She collided with him as he turned.

Sed grabbed hold of her waist to stop her from falling. Diamond melted. Tears were in her eyes as her mind screamed, "No!" She kept her eyes shut.

Sed's hand instinctively went to her cheeks and wiped off the tears. He could not understand why he felt such passion for this woman. He could have any woman he wanted. Earthly women were easy, but this one was obviously struggling. He wondered if it was the drugs affecting her. He sincerely hoped that it was not the drug, but she herself resisting.

However, he knew better. No woman had been able to resist the effects of the drug before. Only strong-will could help a victim. He drew her closer and felt her warmth against his cotton shirt. She was almost burning. He lifted her chin, and their lips were only an inch apart.

A voice echoed into Diamond's soul as clear as if someone suddenly shouted at her: "Flee!" She awoke from her trance, and with the bit of willpower left in her, Diamond pushed Sed away and sprang for the front door.

Sed staggered, letting go of his grip. He had not expected this reaction at all and was shocked. The woman was already out of the house and running into the woods. Sed was now convinced that her system must have flushed out the drugs faster than he had anticipated. The overwhelming emotion made him bow his head. There was an intense surge of adrenalin. His dark side took over. Instead of love, he felt such intense desperation, and he knew that Dracon had been observing all this while, feeding him with darkness. He had to have her at all costs, and now. His blue eyes had turned dark from the darkness. His desire was fed from the rage of PIT. He activated the tracker button on his watch, but there were no coordinates.

"The serum has definitely worn out," he thought.

He still had more in his ring. He pressed a side button on his watch, and a hidden slot opened, exposing an azurite ring. He wore the ring and went after Diamond.

The woman ran through the dark woods. She ran faster than she had ever run in her life.

Meanwhile, Jim woke up with a startle. He

had been dreaming that his wife was being chased by a wild beast that wanted to devour her. He had stretched his hands to help her, and she had tried to reach for his hand but failed. She was falling, and the beast was almost upon her. Jim picked up the phone and dialed her mobile. Nothing. No one picked. He did the only thing he could. He went down on his knees and prayed.

....

Sed's senses became heightened as the darkness fed him. He could smell her, stronger than before. As an entity of the second rank after Dracon, he could control his emotions if he wanted to and override the darkness from PIT. He focused his will on resisting the darkness so that he would not kill the woman. He walked out of the cabin, trailing her scent and controlling his desire to run with the speed of light. His rage was still so intense, and it would take some time before his will completely overrode the darkness. He walked more slowly to expel the darkness before reaching her.

"Maybe Diamond could heal him," he thought.

Diamond turned Southeast and emerged from the woods onto a clearing and road leading further down. Looking behind her, she saw no Sed. She stopped to catch her breath and wiped her eyes with her hands.

"What do I do now?" she thought.

A rustling sound from the woods startled her. She looked in the direction of the sound. Sed stepped out of the woods, causing Diamond to run.

While all this was going on, Blanton waited for his son. He did not have to wait too long. His voice echoed through to him.

"Dad! Dad!" Matthew called out into the dark wood.

"Here," Blanton said quietly and signaled to the young man.

Matthew hugged his father and spoke at the same time, rushing the words.

"Our house, Dad? It's all gone."

"Yes, it is," Blanton replied. "I'm glad you guys are okay."

"So, who is that guy? Matthew inquired.

"Some sort of bionic robot, who can take on any organic or inorganic form he wants," said Blanton.

"An alien?" asked Matthew.

"Not really. They've been here for a very long time, maybe before creation. I'm not sure," Blanton said as he grabbed the young man's hand. "Come. We need to get to work." They went to where the trap was set, and both talked about how they would entrap the Listener.

In the Lodge, Sarah asked the Listener to check up on their son. He tarried too long in returning, and she was worried. The Listener agreed and went to find Matthew. Sarah was happy to have her husband with them. She felt such confidence in him. He had always been an inspiration to her since first seeing him. Her thoughts went to their first meeting as she lay on the bed, awaiting the return of the two men in her life.

They had collided with each other on the stairs of the University of Massachusetts. She was late for an audition, and Blanton was coming out of a lecture. She had bumped into him and knocked off the heap of notes he carried. It was extremely windy, and everything blew away. They spent the next hour running after the notes, and she had missed that audition.

Sarah smiled and drifted off to sleep.

The Listener knew precisely where to find Matthew. He activated his tracking device and received the young man's coordinates. He could also hear his voice.

Diamond stopped running once she approached another Lodge. It was the Hog Hollow Country Lodge. Her legs were already tired. She had covered 900 meters. Only two buildings had their lights on. One was closer to her, and the more prominent building, which looked like an office, was further down. She banged on the door of the closest one.

Sarah was awakened from sleep by a heavy banging sound. She wondered if she had locked the doors and the men were trying to get in. The loud bang continued, and she got up.

Diamond was exhausted. She turned to see

if the man was still after her. He was right there, coming towards her but taking his time. Diamond left the door and ran from the front porch into the woods. Sarah got to the door and opened it. No one was there. She peered outside and saw a man walking and a woman running while constantly looking behind her at the man. She saw the woman disappear into the woods. Sarah sensed danger. She closed the door behind her and went to alert security, wondering why her husband took so long to return.

"Hello," said Sarah to the receptionist.

The receptionist glanced at the wall clock. It was 1:00 a.m., and she responded with surprise.

"Hello, madam. How can I be of help?" said the male receptionist.

"I do not mean to bother you, but I need you to alert your security. I saw a woman running into the woods. She seems to be running from someone, a man," said Sarah, pointing in the direction where she last saw Diamond.

The receptionist smiled and repeated, "A woman running into the woods and chased by a man?" and tried to stifle a chuckle.

"Yes," Sarah said, wondering what could be so funny. "Maybe they are lovers, madam. This is a romantic get-away Lodge," the receptionist tried to explain. "You are the only landlord we have here."

"This did not look romantic at all. She seemed frightened," Sarah responded, sounding angry.

"Okay, ma'am. Please confirm. Was the man holding any weapon?" he asked as nicely as he could.

"Well, it was quite dark. I did not observe that," Sarah said.

"Then, I must insist they are lovers," he said, noting Sarah's expression. "But I'll notify security just in case. I will send someone to the woods to check the sites," he added.

"That'll be great," Sarah said, already walking herself out the door towards the woods. She knew the woods well but had never gone out so late into the night on all their trips.

"If Blanton and Matthew are there, I'll be fine. I wonder what they are up to," she wondered, stepping across a tree stump and entering the woods.

Meanwhile, Sed's rage had diminished as he pursued the woman.

He felt her feebleness and only wanted to hold her in his arms. If she was unmarried, he knew it would have been easier. She would not have run away. He had to get to her and bring her back. Running into the woods at this time of the night was not a good idea.

"I have completely lost her," he said, peering through the trees. He had walked quickly to catch up with her as she was about to enter the woods. He did not risk accelerating for fear of being seen by the woman staring at him. Switching on his scanner, he saw four dots on the watch's screen. One was a stationary orange dot. A green dot was approaching two blue stationary dots. He knew the green had to be Diamond, as it was the only green dot. The color green represented females, while blue signified a male presence. But, the orange color was what disturbed him: A Listener was on site. That would mean death for anyone he encountered. Listeners wouldn't walk on Earth except on a mission to kill. Sed connected to the Listener.

"Why are you here," Sed asked.

"To wipe out 7,632 and all that is related to

him," replied the robot.

Sed knew he could not ask the Listener to abort the mission. Directives came from Band, the War Lord. He looked at his watch's screen. The orange dot was still stationary.

"He must be recharging," Sed thought, looking at the full moon. "Yes, definitely recharging."

Sed had to move now, or it would be too late.

Matthew was about to move from his dad's side when they heard leaves rustling nearby. Startled and afraid, they hid in the woods waiting. A figure emerged from the woods. It stood right in between the tree and the rock trap. There was a snap, and suddenly, twines encircled the figure. A woman screamed.

Sed heard the shrill scream and looked at the screen. The green and blue dots were together. The orange dot had started to move. Transporting himself quickly to the Listener, Sed tried to grab his neck from behind, but the Listener sensed his every move and knew his every thought. Sed drew his lightning sword, the only thing that could disarm a Listener since they could not be killed.

The Listener scanned Sed. "Emotions," he said. "You have emotions, Lord Sed, which have blinded you."

"Abort this mission," Sed commanded.

"Mission must be fulfilled," responded the robot. They both engaged in a fierce battle.

Meanwhile, the two men heard the scream and quickly ran to the woman before she would be flung into space and onto spikes that were sure to kill her.

The rock was already in mid-air, pulled by the firmly knitted vines. Blanton jumped right on top of it and started to cut as fast as he could. Matthew instinctively jumped and held Diamond down with all his weight. Sarah emerged; she had also heard the scream and ran in the direction it came from. The moonlight was bright and illuminated the small opening.

"Matthew? Honey?" she called out as she saw the three figures.

Help me hold her down," Matthew shouted to his mother.

She ran to him.

There was a sudden loud explosion, and a burst of red light occurred two meters to the Northwest from where they struggled. Their grip on the woman loosened, and she was raised into the air 4 feet. Blanton almost fell off the rising rock.

"Hold me, Mom," Matthew screamed as he jumped and caught the screaming woman. Both their weights forced her down. Blanton finally cut the thick vine and jumped off the rock as it was about to hit the ground.

"Are you guys okay?" Blanton asked, some seconds later, as he emerged from the woods. The rock had moved him further away into the woods while in mid-air.

Matthew removed the last vine that was wrapped around Diamond and said, "We are good."

"Are you alright?" Sarah spoke directly to Diamond.

"I'm fine," she responded, looking at the woods as if waiting for something.

"I think he is gone. You don't need to be afraid," Sarah said, following her gaze.

Diamond looked at Sarah, confused.

"You knocked on my door earlier. Some guy was in pursuit."

"Thank you," Diamond said in a faint voice.

Sarah got up to speak with her husband. She saw his unshaven beard and was shocked.

"Blanton?"

"Yes, love. It's me."

Another loud explosion and a red light filled the sky. Something emerged into their space. It was the Listener. Sed had tried to strike him, but his deflecting shield had repelled the seducer's lightning sword, resulting in the second explosion. Sed had been knocked unconscious momentarily.

The Listener, in a split second, grabbed Blanton and his son by their necks and lifted them. He would break their necks and separate their heads from their bodies in a few seconds. Diamond touched the Listener. She was as bright as white light. The ground shook. The whole Earth rumbled, and all lights went out.

CHAPTER FOUR

A POLAR SHIFT

Dracon was in his study, reviewing the reports from the search for 'the one' when the PIT trumpets sounded. He counted 13 metallic and intense blasts.

"The one!" he exclaimed. "Found?"

With the wave of his hand, a screen appeared, and he saw her.

"What! That is 6365!" he exclaimed, staring at the same woman he had seen on Earth, sleeping at the coordinates in Abuja City.

There she was, enveloped in the most brilliant light he had seen since the fall. Dracon became worried.

"How could anyone have such light at this present age?" They had done everything to ensure that all humans believed in an illusion," he thought.

Thirty minutes earlier, before the trumpets sounded, he had observed the Listener's light disappear from his screen and had zoomed in on his coordinates. The image that came up had frightened him.

"No human had been able to disintegrate a Listener before unless those from above heaven," thought Dracon. He had seen the Listener disintegrate at Diamond's touch, and the Ether had opened up to swallow the soul that occupied the bionic body. Pitalunans feared death more than anything, for they were already damned. The Ether was placed above the Earth and only visible at night. He remembered the event that led to its creation and the number of souls already trapped there for all eternity. There was no worse punishment than the Ether. Dracon shook the thoughts off his mind and concentrated on the present.

"I have found 'the one,' and that was what mattered most. I must trigger the great quake. Earth must fall through one more gate, and there would be no going back. If

Earth can descend through the third gate, all connections to heaven will be lost forever. After that, the Earth will fall through the final gate, and PIT can have its elixir to last a lifetime. Thus, no more connection to heaven results in no more death for Pitalunans. 6365 has to die,"

Dracon thought.

He activated the 'find' button, and detailed information about Diamond's history was sent to the grays and the human agent. Deep within the Earth's mantle, the grays received the message. Ten legions were assigned to find her. A well-known celebrity received the alert on his Gressor Luxor Las Vegas Jackpot at the expensive Park Hotel in New York City. He gently tapped the coordinates in the message on his touchscreen. Diamond's image filled the screen. He stared at the dark brown woman and activated his acceptance of the mission.

Dracon was back in the Halo room, ready to activate the quake that would trigger the fall. He focused the halo's lens upon the Earth. The empty space around the halo started to fill up with iron fibers. An iron ball with spikes became woven. Through a graphic representation of the halo within the intergalactic building, he moved the gigantic invisible machine to face the Earth's equator. The rings of the halo hummed violently and were positioned at the eyes. Then, there was silence for about a minute. Dracon pressed a button. A melody began to play. The first ring started to resonate. Its vibration activated the ring next to it, continuing until the last ring resonated. A stream of energy shot forth from the eye of the halo and enveloped the massive iron ball. It was thrust towards Earth with great power, and began its journey towards its programmed coordinates.

....

.

On Earth, Diamond knew. Her mind opened up to knowledge, wisdom, and understanding, such as she never knew existed. She saw the beginning of time, creation, and everything that had ever been. She understood why everything was and the goal of existence. She knew what must now be done. Coming out of her trance, she looked at her illuminated body. She looked at the men and women staring at her in shock and amazement.

"It is you," said Blanton. "I have found you," he said as he looked up from where he knelt, holding his family in protection.

"Blanton," Diamond called. "Something is coming upon the Earth, and there is no time to ask questions or answer them. It will change life as we know it, but there is hope."

"What is happening, Dad? Who is this woman and ..., asked Matthew? Diamond interrupted.

"It's okay, Matthew. All will be well in no time," Diamond said.

They heard voices approaching the woods. Power was restored, and they could hear several people speaking simultaneously.

"Blanton, you must get to your daughter now and stay with your family. We have only three days before it hits," said Diamond.

"What is going to hit?" Blanton asked, standing from his kneeling position. His wife got up also and held on to him, dragging Matthew along.

"A great iron rock. But it won't be the end," responded Diamond. Her brilliance had gone, and she looked very much human again.

"We have to warn others," said Blanton as footsteps approached.

The voices reached them. Five men in security uniforms emerged from the woods into the opening space. Both groups stared at each other.

"We are fine," Blanton quickly said.

"We saw strange fire and explosion come from this side," said one of the men as he looked around suspiciously.

"We heard it too. What could have caused it?" Blanton asked.

The men looked at each other and shrugged.

"But you are all unhurt, right? said the man who spoke before. He looked like the boss.

"Yes, we all are," Blanton replied.

The security man looked as if he was about to ask more questions but instead said, "We will go further into the woods and search.

Please go back to your cabins," he said as they stepped into the woods and out of site.

"Right away," responded Blanton, holding onto his wife and son's hands, prompting them to move.

"My lady?" he directed at Diamond. I think you should come to our cabin.

"Diamond," she corrected.

"Diamond?" said Blanton, looking confused.

"My name is Diamond," she replied.

They walked towards the cabin and saw Jenny outside, asking someone if he had seen her family and describing them.

"Jenny!" her dad called to her.

She looked at the direction of the voice. "Dad! Mum!"

She ran to her family and hugged everyone at the same time. "I was so worried," she said. "Where were you guys?" asked Jenny. "The light went off, and it was so dark. I called and called, then the explosions. No. The explosions woke me up. I called and called, then it went dark," she said, trying to get out the words all at once

"Calm down, Jenny. What's good is that we are all fine," said Blanton as they entered their cabin.

Blanton gently pulled at Diamond's hand to get her attention and said, "We need to talk."

"In good time, responded Diamond.

"No. I need some real explanations," said Sarah immediately. "What is going on here? Sarah asked her husband in desperation, turning to face him.

"Sarah!" Blanton said and tried to pull her into his arms.

"No. Don't touch me. Why were you with clean-shaven beards and suddenly not? Why is someone trying to kill us? Oh my God! I was with a stranger for two days, or are you the stranger?"

Blanton held her. She struggled and beat against his chest. "What is happening?" Sarah cried out.

"The world is about to end," said Matthew in a cold, careless voice.

"The world is not about to end. If we all sit down, the lady here and I, Diamond, right? Diamond nodded to confirm.

"Yes. Diamond and I will take turns to explain everything."

Everyone sat. Blanton remained standing. "Great. I'll start," said Blanton.

....

Meanwhile, Jim wondered what could have caused the power to go out in Abuja. It had been pitch black for 10 minutes, and the twins were so scared. He had successfully put them back to sleep. He remembered the dream that made him jump up from sleep to pray for his wife. It was while praying that the lights went off.

"Thank God power is back on," he said as he pressed the T.V's power remote button. He dropped the remote on the center table and went to the kitchen to get a glass of water. The DSTV had finished calibrating and the voice of a news reporter blasted loudly over the speakers.

Jim ran back to the living room to turn down the volume. He spilled some of the water. The headline on the screen read

Global Power shut down. What caused this?

He listened.

The 10-minute global power shutdown has caused a lot of chaos and confusion. There has never been such intense pitch darkness

for the duration of the outage. Nothing seems to be wrong with most countries' main power grid. So, what could have caused this? Casualties have been reported from all over the world of patients undergoing procedures during the outage. Backup power did not respond automatically and did not also respond to all manual efforts.

Jim instinctively dashed into his bedroom to get his mobile phone. He had to find out how Diamond was faring.

....

Back in South Africa, Blanton's family were shocked at his words.
"It sounded too much like a science fiction. Matthew had expressed. Diamond's explanation frightened them even more.

"Is this the end of the world?" Jenny asked.

It would definitely be the end of many people and the old system. The world will unite into one, but this will not save humanity. It is the very grand plan of man's enemy."

"How are we going to survive the quake?" Blanton asked as he slowly sat down. What he had just heard weakened his legs.

"Through faith". Make sure you are together, and no matter what you see or what happens, I'm sure there is hope," said Diamond confidently.

"I have to get back to my family in Nigeria. The conference will no longer hold. There will be too many incidents starting tomorrow afternoon,"Diamond said, looking at the scared family.

She looked at the clock on the wall, which was 2:00 am, and said, "If you must go back to your country, you have to do so now, for the hit will be greatest here."

"How about you and your family? Your country is right on the equator," Blanton asked.

"I know, but I have to see them once more before I commence my journey," she responded.

Blanton remembered the message from Igdaleah, which he had conveyed to her during his narration of the past events to his family. He wondered how she would commence a journey to the place above the Ether without being detected by the Pitalunans or what means of transport would take her. He wondered if she was afraid.

Diamond turned to go. Sarah's voice stopped her.

"Wait!" Sarah called to her.

She paused momentarily. Sarah gave her a surprise hug. "This must be such a burden.

I hope you succeed. We all hope you succeed," Sarah said, looking back at her family.

"Thanks. I hope so, too," Diamond said and smiled.

"We won't be going back to Massachusetts. There are too many skyscrapers, and the city is bustling and crowded. If the quake will be as terrible as you described, we will stay here," she said and looked at Blanton for approval.

"Yes. We will," said Blanton, nodding as he stood up.

"Then go to the mountains nearby. You can commence your journey when it's daylight. Rent a Jeep. Take enough food to last you for several weeks and take warm clothing and make-shift beds," said Diamond.

She took some steps towards the front door and stopped as her hands were about to touch the knob. She turned to face Blanton and said, "Please encourage your family when the time comes. They will need it."

Diamond left the bewildered family and jogged to her cabin. She felt such a surge of energy and a boost of health than she had ever felt in her life. She reached Sed's apartment, paused momentarily, and immediately went into a trance. Sed was in a wormhole that went down into the Earth. He was shortly in a place she had never seen before. Suddenly, he was in chains inside a dungeon. A monstrous creature whipped him continuously with metal rods. Sed cried out. The trance changed to another scene. He lay on a flat metal table, and tubes were connected to his head to re-program his mind.

The trance stopped. It frightened her. She suddenly felt drained and walked the rest of the way to her cabin. She reached her front door and heard her phone ringing. It was

Jim's ringtone.

"Hello, love," Diamond said into the phone.

Diamond!" Jim said, with worry heavy in his voice.

"He hardly calls me by name unless he was worried to death about me," thought Diamond.

"I'm fine, love," Diamond said. She did not feel like she used to. It felt weird talking to him. Her mind went to the twins.

"How are David and Daisy?" she asked.

"Very fine, and you? Did you experience the blackout?"

"Yes. It happened here also, but no incidents. I'm bringing my flight forward."

"What about the conference?" Jim asked.

"I need to come back home, love," she responded.

"If you are so sure," said Jim.

"Yes, I am sure," she said, flipping open the laptop on the table.

She checked the flight details and airlines that were not fully booked for that morning's flights to Nigeria. The screen showed numerous options.

"Lots of people are not flying this morning. No flight is fully booked," she said.

"Okay. What time so I could pick you up at the airport?" Jim asked.

"I'll take the 6:30 am flight," she responded.

"That's great then," said Jim.

"Great! I've booked the flight," exclaimed Diamond.

....

On PIT, Sed was back in his palatial building. Dracon could not de-rank him as the King could not strip him of his natural gifts. They had tried to strip him of his emotions and had succeeded. He had more hate for humans than he ever had before.

His new duty was to possess the human agent and capture Diamond. He would not wait until after the quake to begin his mission. Dracon had requested the mission commence immediately because so many truths would be revealed to humans if they waited until after the earthquake, and this was not yet to be.

"You cannot chase such a woman around the Earth, and truths won't be revealed. But during the quake, humans would be too interested in survival than to worry about some mysterious events and sightings," thought Sed, preparing to possess the celebrity.

The celebrity gulped down what was left of the expensive champagne straight from its bottle. He hated the feeling of being possessed and usually tried to get drunk as much as possible before the possession. He laughed.

"If any of my fans see me like this, I don't think I'll be as cool as before. My fans would turn zero," he thought.

The air around him became cold. He flung aside the bottle. It hit the wall in a loud shatter. It was time, and he was ready. He stood in the middle of the circular sign on the floor. It was the image of the halo. He stood on the eye, naked—the price he had to pay for his fame.

Sed, on the other hand, also hated possessing humans. He had always gone on missions in his own body. Dracon had insisted, as part of his punishment, that he used this man's body so that his emotions would not resurface since he would not have direct contact with the woman but would instead go through this body. He stood inside the transporter and was beamed onto the halo world. His spirit hovered right above the eye; a red energy beam encircled him, and he began to spin faster and faster. On Earth, the human agent began to spin, too. A soft symphony started to play. A beam of energy was shot down to Earth with Sed's spirit, and the human agent's spirit was shot into the halo above and encased in a ball.

Sed opened his eyes. He smelt the stink of alcohol. He felt nauseated and vomited on the floor.

"For him, there was no greater punishment than this," Sed thought as he went into the bathroom to shower.

....

Diamond walked through the arrival session of the Nnamdi Azikiwe International Airport. Jim and the kids were right there, waiting for her. She still did not feel the same way. She felt like she did not belong on Earth. Nevertheless, she was pleased to see her family. When they saw their mum, the kids ran to embrace her.

"Oh mum, I've missed you," said David, hugging her legs front the front.

"I've missed you so much, Mum," said Daisy, hugging her from the back.

Diamond laughed, trying to hug both of them at the same time.

"I love you guys, and I've missed you too. But I've only been gone for three days," she gently patted their heads.

"It felt like a million years," they both replied.

"It felt that way for me too. Come to think of it. Hmm. Okay! Okay! Let me hug your dad," Diamond said, unsuccessfully trying to pull her legs free.

The twins refused to leave, and Jim hugged

everyone instead.

"Glad to have you back, love," he said, giving her a peck on the right cheek.

He noticed her worried eyes but decided to mention it later.

"Guys, stop hugging mummy. Let's get home, then you can continue to hug her," their dad said, grabbing onto her single luggage.

The twins reluctantly left her legs.

"Now that mummy is back, we can eat water-yam porridge," said David

"And Ofada rice with stew," Daisy said. Both parents laughed.

"Oh! So, that's why you guys miss mummy," Jim commented.

"Are you trying to say that my food tastes horrible?" he asked as he opened the boot of their Mercedes car.

"Not really," said Daisy.

"Just not as sweet as mummy's food. We

have had only rice and spaghetti every-y-y day-y," said David, dragging his words to emphasize his feelings.

"Come on, guys, get into the car. I'm sure daddy's food was not that bad," their mum said, laughing as she closed the back door after they had gotten in.

"I heard everything. So, no more trips for you guys," their dad teased.

"Your spaghetti tastes great, Dad," David quickly said.

"The rice also. Just that we miss ofada and water yam porridge," Daisy said.

"Maybe mummy and I will engage in a cooking competition. The best cook will win the cook of the year," said Jim as he drove the car through the turn that linked to the highway.

The kids laughed. Their parents joined in.

"Sure," Diamond said. "Hopefully," she said in her mind.

When they arrived home, Diamond was treated to a nice meal of steaming hot spaghetti prepared by Jim. It tasted great. The kids were not hungry and had gone into the game room instead. Diamond and Jim sat in the living room.

"So?" Jim said, looking at Diamond expectantly. "So what?" she asked, looking unsure.

"So, I'm waiting to hear why you rushed back home," said Jim.

"Phew!" Diamond sighed and said, "So many things happened in South Africa, love. You know the dreams I've been having?"

"Yeah? What about them?"

"Some have already happened, and one is about to happen that would change the world as we know it," she responded as she got up to sit closer to him.

"Here we go again with those dreams, love. Okay, what is about to happen?"

"Honestly, I don't think I should bother you with the details."

"Please bother me with the details. You rushed back to Nigeria from S.A. without a tangible explanation, throwing away a once-in-a-lifetime opportunity. I don't understand you at all, and I'm not too happy about this. You have become a different person since you started having dreams," Jim said, his face in a frown.

"My exact point, love. I'm a different person now, and I do not know how to explain everything that has happened or is about to happen. But one thing is certain: there will be a massive global earthquake any minute now, and Africa will be the most hit."

Jim looked at her queerly and then laughed.

"I don't believe this. If China or somewhere else that is earthquake-prone, then I'll believe this, but in Africa! Maybe North

Africa. We've not had a single earthquake in the last thousand years in West Africa, and you are talking about a global earthquake occurring any minute from now. Where are the tremors? At least, we should have started seeing those. So, I don't get this. Also, we've had floods in several places, tornadoes and earthquakes in the USA, and quakes in Asia and the Middle East, but not Africa. Only famine and flooding is prominent here."

"Jim?" Diamond called his name, trying to pause him so that she could speak.

"Wait! I agree that the intensity of natural disasters has heightened over the years, but a global earthquake? No. That would require something half the weight of the Earth to strike it."

Diamond decided not to argue; she knew her husband would disagree. How could he accept that his wife, the mother of his kids, was more than she appeared, could see other worlds, and knew everything from the beginning of creation up to their present time?

"I'm too tired, Jim. I think I'll do the dishes now and go to bed."

He looked at her. His face was still drawn in a frown. She watched the frown slowly melt into a smile.

"Alright. No problem. Let me assist you."

"No! No! I'm fine. I'll wash them. You cooked. So, I'll wash. Thanks a bunch."

Jim realized he was also tired.

"Okay then. I guess I'll listen to the news," he said, looking outside through the drawn window blind in the living room. "It looks like we are going to have rain. It's becoming cloudy and dark."

"Yeah. It looks that way. I'll quickly do the dishes and join you."

"Thought you wanted to sleep," he

reminded her.

"Yes. In your arms and wherever you are," she responded, smiling.

"The twins will catch us cuddling," he warned.

"They are big kids now, love. We won't be cuddling, I'll be sleeping with my head on your laps and you'll be sitting on the couch, watching T.V. That's not cuddling."

"Yeah, and a little bit of cuddling," Jim teased.

"Yeah!" she responded with her back turned while climbing the short steps that linked the corridor to the kitchen.

Jim switched on the T.V and changed the channel to the Local news station.

"Nothing, no natural disasters today. Just lots of rain to be expected," he said to himself.

He switched the channel to an International news station and watched for several minutes.

"No disasters this month. A few tornadoes, some floods, and low magnitude quakes. No causalities. Good," he said.

Then suddenly,

"Breaking News: CASA has discovered an asteroid on a collision course with Earth. It is possible it might not hit Earth but nevertheless, we should all pray. This was not discovered by the most powerful telescope until about an hour ago. We have invited Scientist Shabam Blum to explain more details about this."

Jim sat upright. "There have been several asteroids on collision courses with Earth before, but they have always turned out to be near-misses. How can this one be any different," he thought.

"Welcome, Mr. Blum."

"Thank you for having me."

"Please, can you shed more light on this sudden, unexpected event that is about to happen? Should we be worried about a collision, or would it be just another near-miss?"

"Well, it is likely to be another near-miss. This one was not discovered early because it belongs to the family of dark asteroids that remain usually unseen until they are very close to the Earth. Such has happened before, and we did not have an impact. So, I'll say no need to worry yourselves about an apocalyptic end of the Earth."

"Yes, but what about a scenario where the asteroid does hit the Earth?" the reporter asked. "Would there be any hope for survival? What can people do in such a situation?"

Jim wondered why Diamond was taking so long to do the dishes.

"Well, if the asteroid does hit the Earth, then it would be a cataclysm of heightened natural disasters. Intensified enough to wipe out one-third of the Earth and render the globe back to the stone ages. There is nothing anyone can do but wait for everything to calm down. Maybe those with underground bunkers will fare well. But the surface would not be a welcome place for any living thing. Except maybe the amoebas or so, but even those will be affected to a high level. We should expect global floods and volcanoes. Global earthquakes and others," responded Blum.

"Wow! That seems scary. We hope it's just another near-miss. Thank you so much for coming on this show, Mr. Blum."

"Thank you for having me."

"Well, we heard it all. Thank you for listening. Back to you, Mike."

"Another near-miss, I'm sure," Jim said to himself, reclining on the sofa. "I guess I'll start the sleeping for her."

Diamond had finished washing the dishes but decided to wash the fridge and the oven and clean up the whole kitchen. She was feeling somewhat restless. She noticed the rain cloud become darker, but not windy outside. It would have become windy in Abuja when such a cloud appeared in daylight. It meant a heavy, windy thunderstorm, plus lots of rain, but never enough to cause a flood. Abuja had a very efficient and standard drainage system, unlike other cities in the country.

The room temperature changed without warning and in a split second. It was hot—very hot. Diamond sprinted from the kitchen towards the children's room, screaming her husband's name as she did.

"JIM!" It has started.

Jim jumped up. He had already dozed off. His shirt was sweaty, and he wondered if he had slept until night. It was so dark, and the T.V was still on.

"JIM!" Diamond screamed again. She had grabbed the thick blankets from off the bed, dipped them in the water basins, and thrown some ice cubes into the basin. The twins were with her and crying. She ignored the crying.

"Just follow me everywhere I go," she commanded her kids. "JIM! It has started. We have to go now."

An enormous roar from outside startled them all. Jim was fully awake now. It was intensely hot. A massive ball of fire was approaching them. It covered the whole sky, and the clouds burned. Diamond quickly grabbed Daisy.

"Carry David," she barked at him.

Jim sprang into action and lifted the crying boy. He followed his wife. She entered the big, wide, cold basin with Daisy. Jim dropped David into the basin and entered, too. They covered themselves with the thick blankets and waited. Another loud roar and the asteroid hit the ground. It hit the beautiful city, and a massive plume of smoke, dust, and sand displaced into the atmosphere. It was dark in the basin. Their heads were under the water. They held their breath. The twins did not understand what was happening but were very cooperative. They were too scared to do anything else. The noise outside was so loud and strange. Diamond began to glow. Jim and the Kids started to scream and ran out of the basin, thinking that the basin was burning. Diamond held Jim's hand and pulled him back. She stood up and grabbed Daisy.

"We have to go now, do not be afraid. The Creator has assured me that we will be alright," she said to the frightened group.

Jim and the kids were in shock, but the fire outside was not a place they could run to. Everyone was silent and obeyed Diamond. A blast of hot air shattered the apartment windows and rushed at them. The basin melted before their eyes, and the water evaporated in a steam. There was screaming. Eyes were closed. Then silence.

Jim opened his eyes. They were still there. Two meters away, the ground had opened, and lava was streaming out of the open crevice. He was not hurt. He looked at his kids. Everyone was unhurt, and Diamond was still glowing brilliant white. He carried David in his arms.

"Let's go," he said.

Diamond carried Daisy, and they left the crumbling apartment.

It was dark outside. There was non-stop screaming. Jim jumped across the magma-filled fracture, and Diamond followed.

"We have to go to the mountain," she said, pointing to the nearby rock. That's the one I saw in my dreams."

"Anything you say," David responded.

The ground shook suddenly, and more crevices opened, spewing out lava. Two men by their side fell in.

"We have to hurry. Follow me," shouted Diamond amidst the loud sound coming out of the sky. They ran, jumping over lava. The ground was quickly becoming covered by an increasing river of flowing magma. It was as if they were in her dream, and she remembered their pathway to escape doom. It was right there before her. Diamond stepped onto the bushy winding path just as the Earth beneath where she stood a moment ago disappeared into a deep but narrow gorge. It was hard to stand due to the quaking Earth. Jim quickly jumped over with David as the gorge widened to more than a kilometer wide, the Earth crumbling beneath their feet as they ran. The twins kept screaming. They got to the foot of the mountain. Several people had followed them upon seeing an illuminated being. They started to climb. The magma turned to a sea of hot spewing molten rock and covered the whole city. They kept climbing with the people following. The sea of lava surrounded the rock. They got to the top and waited. It continued to rise until it was a kilometer away and stopped. Everyone crowded together and waited. Diamond looked to her left. There was a building atop the mountain. She could see every room in the building in a vision - stacked with food, beds, and warm clothing but unoccupied.

The asteroid hit the city around 2:00 pm that afternoon, and it was already 8:00 pm. The dust from the impact loomed all over the Earth and shunned the sun's light. The fracture that was caused by the impact weakened other fault lines, and there were massive quakes in several cities. Electricity was no more. All volcanic rocks had become active within hours of the impact. A gigantic tsunami covered all coastal areas, with only one-third of South America remaining in the Americas. Africa had burnt up with only Diamond and the survivors with her left. The Middle East was untouched, and the Asian continent had been divided in half, with only one-fifth of the half that was the Balkans, not covered by the sea. Australia was no more. Europe had vanished entirely, and the United

Kingdom had broken into numerous islands.

Back in what remained of Abuja, where Diamond was, the sea of magma had stopped rising. The air around the building was clean and pure. It was nothing short of a miracle. Diamond stood on the flat roof and looked at the horizon. It was still dark. Very dark. It's been about thirty days since the impact, and the world before her was unrecognizable. No building or any other structure or form in site. All was molten lava, as if the Earth had been cleansed. But Diamond knew better. It was only a matter of time before they came for her. But what was she to do when they showed? The answer to this question eluded her. She went back inside the room they had picked in the building. It was tastefully furnished and untouched. She wondered how only this place could have been spared. The kids looked tired and about to sleep. She watched them for a while. Their dad played the tickle game, so they would not sleep yet.

"I guess it's time for bed, right?" she asked.

The kids were still laughing. Their dad was tickling them.

"I guess so, said Jim as he looked up at his wife. He was kneeling on the floor.

"Our guardian angel is back," David said.

"She is our mummy, not a guardian angel," Daisy corrected gently.

"I am still your mummy. Hmm? Let's prepare for bed."

In no time, the kids were asleep. Jim held his wife but was afraid to make love to her. She had recounted everything that happened in South Africa, including the episode with Sed after they had been on the mountain for about a week. He kept wondering if she was human or not. If touching her that way would change anything about her. He wanted his wife, but in the present situation on Earth, he preferred she remained untouched so she could glow when it was time to glow. Diamond was fast asleep. She breathed softly and slept sweetly. Jim was soon fast asleep.

The Earth turned. The North Pole became South, and the South Pole became North. A rapidly flowing icy wind approached from the West and rapidly froze everything it touched. The magma quickly cooled, and everything it touched on the Earth froze instantaneously, but the mountain and its occupants were sound asleep. New Zealand was also spared.

CHAPTER FIVE

THE CHASE AND THE FINAL CYCLE

Suspended in the air, above the halo, was a massive cauldron. Human souls encased in energy balls traveled in a wormhole into the cauldron, which had a purple sticky-aqueous suspension. The elixir of PIT was being prepared—a mixture of violence, misery, and the purple catalyst.

Dracon was glad. "There was no way 'the one' could have escaped all that; if she had, it would still be easy to destroy her. No earthling would care if the Pitulanans showed up now. They were too busy covered in misery and depression after losing everything they had ever known, including loved ones," thought Dracon. He remembered what it was like after the great flood. They had left Earth at that time and left their human wives behind. After the floods were decreased, and thought their wives dead, they helped rebuild the human world. They ensured that the truth was still covered, but later on discovered that the dolphins had helped the women they left behind and were now caricatures of what a human and fish would look like when fused together. They were half fish and half women. The wives had begged Dracon to take them back, but he had refused. He could not bear to live with such disfigurement and had confined them to the deepest parts of the sea, where no human ship or submarine could ever go. Instead, tales of beautiful mermaids was programmed into the human mind, but the reality was far from this. He remembered how their children had been banned to a land far away and separated from the Earth by sea, then a desert of solid ice that no man could cross, either by foot, flight, or ship, followed by a desert of sinking ice, which was more comprehensive than the desert of solid ice. His first son had also been deformed. He was a hybrid of part-human and part-goat, and Dracon had been very angry. The child and others born like him had such an appetite for human flesh that they regretted having human wives, but nothing could be done now. The only thing was to ban them to a desolate island and feed them through the various human disappearances and kidnappings that filled the news. He had suffered more than these humans could imagine, and he was not ready to allow them to learn about all this. He would kill them all and leave no single soul on Earth.

His mind returned to the present. The cauldron was three times bigger than the Earth and already half full.

"This is enough to rebuild and sustain PIT for another thousand years," Dracon thought. Another quake and the Earth will finally drop, never to rise again, and I will have a claim and right to rule it forever," he said, laughing as he watched the moon turn blood red. This was a sign that the Earth had fallen yet through another gate—the fourth gate.

....

Back on Earth, Diamond woke up first. She felt well-rested after the long sleep. She could not tell for how long but was sure it was long enough. She tapped Jim.

"Wake up, love. I think it is morning."

"Uhm? Morning? Okay," Jim answered, sounding drowsy, and stretched himself while yawning. He dozed off again.

"Wake up, sleepy head," Diamond tapped him again.

"I'm up. See! My eyes are wide open now," he said, with his fingers on his eyelids, pulling them apart to stretch them open.

"I'll be outside," Diamond said, stepping out of the room to observe if the volcanic ash was still burning.

"Okay. I'll join you in a bit," Jim answered back. Diamond took a walk around the building to check on the other survivors. She had become stronger each day. She noticed that her movements and reflexes were faster than usual. A walk that would have taken up to 5 minutes was now completed in 5 seconds. She didn't understand what was happening to her but loved it nevertheless. She opened the building's main exit door and stepped outside. It was white beyond the radius of a kilometer from where she stood. She walked on the exposed rock until she reached the point where the ice started. She gently stepped on the ice. It was cold, but not so cold that she could not walk on it.

She stepped even further away from the building. She could see that the ground still had deep crevices but no magma. All had been frozen solid.

"Diamond!"

She heard Jim's voice call out to her. Diamond turned to face him. He was hitting against an invisible wall. Diamond did not understand. She walked back towards the building and placed her hand opposite his palm. Their hands touched, but Jim could not cross to her side. She crossed to his side and placed her palm beside Jim's. It went straight through while Jim's palm was stopped by an invisible barrier. He hit the barrier again and again.

"It seems there is an invisible force field here that only you can pass through. Maybe that's what prevented the magma and the ice from reaching us in the building," Jim said as he pulled her closer, afraid that if she crossed again, the force field might not allow her to come back."

Meanwhile, an alarm had gone off deep in the Earth's mantle. The grays had been searching for Diamond for over 30 days. Immediately after she stepped out of the perimeter of the force field, their satellite detected her and sent the message to the grays. Sed also received the same message and immediately activated the transporter to the coordinates he had received. Diamond saw a silvery ladder appear 13 feet from where the ice started. Jim saw it, too.

"What's that?" he asked, pointing to the silvery but old-looking ladder. His gaze followed it up to the heavens, where it disappeared from sight.

"My journey has begun, Jim. I have to go. Please take care of our children. I do not know when I'll return. Whatever happens, do not leave this place. You and the children," said Diamond.

The noise of a spaceship made her stop talking. It hovered 26 meters away from where she stood.

"Who are those?" Jim asked in a whisper.

"The grays," she answered.

"The grays?"

What are those?" he inquired.

"They are here to capture me," she said.

Jim looked at his wife. She did not seem the least troubled. He held her hand.

An ashen-looking figure walked down the steps that extended from the hovering ship onto the Earth. He walked towards them, as if he could not see them or the building. He tapped on the force field, and it sounded like the surface of hard-sold granite.

The gray mumbled something in a foreign language.

"What did he say," Jim asked.

"Just a solid wall of rock covered in ice," Diamond responded.

The couple looked at each other surprised.

"So, you can understand every language now. Wow!" Jim exclaimed, surprised.

"I guess so," Diamond responded, staring at the gray who turned and returned to the ship. It still hovered at the same position.

The ladder began to fade. Diamond knew she had to go now, or it would be too late.

She turned and quickly hugged Jim.

"I love you," she said, whispering in his ears and stepped out.

Jim saw her move with lightning speed towards the ladder. The gray stopped walking and turned quickly. The alarm had gone off again. He saw her and was filled with so much hate. He had to delay her so that the ladder could vanish.

Sed's alarm went off again. He quickly launched the transporter, which traveled at lightning speed. He had waited a second too long before and the coordinates disappeared. He was not going to delay this time around. He had to finish his mission.

Diamond was just a meter to the ladder. It had almost faded completely. The gray was a meter and a half away. They were both on opposite sides of the ladder. In the half of a split second, Diamond reached the ladder. The gray reached it and almost grabbed her legs. Diamond knew they must not touch her. She climbed as fast as she could. The transporter rematerialized Sed, just steps below the gray, just as it disappeared.

Jim watched on. He saw his wife and her pursuers disappear. He felt both angry and helpless. A voice made him jolt in fright.

"Dad, what are you looking at?" David asked, tapping on his father's leg.

Jim bent over to match the boys' height and responded while holding him tightly to hide his tear-filled eyes.

"Just the snow, love. Just the snow," he said.

"Where is mummy? asked David.

He stood up and lifted the young boy in his arms.

"I will tell you soon. It's cold out here," he responded, walking back towards the building.

Diamond was aglow again. This time, more than she had ever been. She climbed even faster, feeling stronger as she did. The gray was losing her. He had not expected 'the one' to be this strong or fast. He knew he could not go past the sky that was visible to human eyes and must stop her before her bright hands touched the first ceiling. With all his mental power, the gray tried to create a powerful illusion. Diamond sensed his plan and shot a burst of energy from her right palm toward the gray. He screamed as the light hit him. A wormhole opened, and he was sucked into the Ether. Sed dodged to the right, avoiding the blast.

The sky above her became bright due to the brilliance emanating from her. She looked down. The stratosphere below was not affected by the volcanic ash and dust. It was clear, blue, and peaceful. Sed was almost closing in. She looked up; the sky above her swayed like a molten surface. She touched it, and it felt solid. She remembered her dream and gave the surface a hard punch. A cracking sound emanated from the ceiling. Just in time, she gave it another punch and climbed through the punctured hole. She felt stronger and became brighter. Her speed increased. In front of her was a ring-shaped world encircling the sun.

Diamond passed through the world like a shooting star, still ascending the ladder. She broke the ceiling of that world and continued until she reached the 8th ringworld. She broke through and climbed out. She was atop the plateau of the highest mountain in the world. She knew its name, but it was not Everest. Nothing was in sight but the Ether; she felt thick darkness. She ran and came to an immediate halt at the plateau's edge. The edge dropped sharply into a deep gorge. She could see only darkness from where she stood. She walked back to the hole she had emerged from and looked down. No one followed. She was all alone. Diamond waited. Nothing happened. Silence and the Ether were all she could see. Diamond became angry at the deceit of humanity and the helplessness of it all.

"What now?" she screamed angrily at the Ether. She began to cry.

"I have come this far for what? To this nothingness? I have left everything I love behind. Why?"

She got up from the plateau and again walked to the edge to observe.

"Maybe there was something she was missing," she thought.

She looked ahead, as far as her eyes could allow, and saw a faint silver lining, far away across the gorge. It was the end of the deep gap. She remembered her dreams and felt abashed.

"The golden gate!" she exclaimed. "I have to get to the golden gate," she said aloud, looking around for a ladder or anything she was supposed to use.

"Nothing!" she said quietly and tried stepping onto the space, hoping that maybe she would be able to walk over the gorge. Her feet did not touch anything solid.

"I can't do this," she said amidst more tears

and tried again.

"Wait!" a voice said calmly but sharply.

Diamond almost fell off and struggled to balance herself back onto the plateau. The voice sounded familiar. She turned slowly. An old woman sat in a wheelchair in the middle of the blue glowing plateau.

"Do not despair, Diamond. You have gotten this far and must not give up now. You have to go on," said the woman kindly. "You have to jump off this firmament and believe as you jump.

"Jump? Diamond echoed in disbelief. "Yes. Jump."

"There is nothing there. The silver line is too far. No one can jump that, and the Ether looks like it would pull me down if I tried."

"Maybe and maybe not Diamond. Would you instead go back?

Diamond did not respond.

"You cannot. Would you rather stay here and waste away like I have been wasting away? I refused to jump because of fear, and here I am."

Diamond felt pity for the woman.

"We can jump together," Diamond said, kneeling beside the woman on the cold, glowing blue firmament.

"No, Diamond," said the woman harshly, pushing her away. "You have to jump now. Think about your family. You have to jump now."

As if prompted by the push, Diamond walked to the cliff's edge. She made up her mind.

"I'll jump," she said determinedly.

She took a few steps backward, ran towards the cliff's edge as fast as possible, and jumped. No sooner had both feet lifted off the firmament and into the air than she heard the sound of a horse. A white brilliant winged horse caught her on its back in mid-air. She recollected a forgotten and strange memory of her horse and the times they had spent together. She knew the horse's name and felt connected to it. The horse flew her over the gorge towards the silver lining. As they got closer, she saw the beautiful plain. It was covered in soft green grass. The color looked intense and more real than any green she had ever seen. It looked pure and undiluted; neither was it blemished. The brilliant white horse got to the plain, and Diamond gently alighted. She was filled with such joy. The golden gate was before her. The gate reached higher than her eyes could see. Diamond looked back at the gorge and towards the dark expanse. Her horse was nowhere in sight, and neither could she see any sign of the firmament. She started to walk towards the gate and felt a presence coming fast from behind. It was the Ether. Diamond ran, certain that it would not be able to cross over to the field. She was wrong. Diamond ran towards the gate with all her might.

"What if the gate does not open for me? What if I am not worthy to knock upon the door," she thought as she ran.

The Ether was only an arm's length away—a cloud of darkness that could be felt. Inside were the souls of the fallen ones who had died. Diamond reached the gate. A male in the image of a man was standing there. He opened the massive gate and pulled her inside as the Ether was about to touch her. The gate closed.

Dracon was in a rage. "All had failed him," he thought. I must activate the last cycle before it's too late."

He activated his transporter. He would do this from the world above to have the most effective result. Earth must not be lost to him. He started to sing the symphony of cataclysm. A song, known only to the worlds that were situated above the halo eye. Soon, he dissipated from sight and reappeared in his throne room. Without wasting time, he beamed all the energy gathered over the years from the artificial worlds and Earth towards the eye of the halo. A beam shot from the eye onto a massive star beneath the Earth. The star began to collapse onto itself to form a black hole that would pull Earth into PIT. Diamond appeared above the halo world. It was a ring structure with eight tentacles spread out on each side. The structure of an eye was in the middle. Two tentacles of worlds protruded from the North and South of the circle, another two from the East and West of the Circle. Four other worlds ran diagonally, facing the

North-East, North-West, South-East, and South-West directions. These were shorter than those on the main poles. Eight planets encircled the end of each tentacle. She knew their names.

Diamond focused her mind on the control room and appeared there. She saw Dracon and focused her mind on the star. She appeared under the star. With a swing from her flaming sword, Diamond swung with all her might at the star. Like a tennis ball, the star was displaced and moved with lightning speed towards the eye, breaking the ringworlds as it went. Dracon saw it coming and drew more energy into the beam to dissipate the approaching star. The star hit the eye, and a loud explosion followed. Diamond created an energy beam around herself as bits and pieces of space rock flew past. The firmament cracked open and began to disintegrate.

It had been 500 years since Diamond left the Earth. Ten seconds in heaven equates to 100 years on Earth. Humans had rebuilt the world, and another civilization was already in existence. Those who survived on the mountain had lost the genome that caused death.

Jim looked into the heavens from his crystal mansion, built upon the very rock that had saved them. He had built a powerful telescope there. He looked nothing like a man of 540 years.

"Can you see her dad?" David asked, now a young adult aged 510.

"No son. Nothing," responded Jim.

"Do you think she made it? David asked.

"I hope so," responded Jim.

The clouds began to dissipate and eventually disappeared. Someone looked up from the streets. There was a visible crack in the bright blue sky. The crack began to spread, and the person screamed, pointing up. Others looked and started to scream. The whole world was thrown into confusion once again. There was nowhere to run from a falling sky.

Jim looked up and saw the crack.

"Time to activate the shield," he said to David.

"Okay, Dad," David said and ran to the basement.

They had constructed an earth shielder machine after Jim dreamed of the firmament falling.

David pressed the button, and an energy beam shot up into the sky from the mountain's top. It spread from the equator to the ends of the Earth. The firmament shattered, and everything fell. All the satellites, the eight-ringed worlds, and the halo worlds fell, burning up as they hit the hot, burning firmament. It was a frightful sight for the survivors on Earth and continued for eight months until the humans got used to it.

Diamond woke up. She was beside her husband on a crystalline bed. She tapped the sleeping man.

David stirred. He had dreamt every night that Diamond returned, tapping him on the shoulder. He sprang up, and there she was.

THE END

About The Author

"My passion for writing started at 8 when, out of boredom, I picked up my pencil and wrote my first poem. Daddy was my first audience. May God bless his soul. He laughed heartily after reading the poem. It was more of a paradox about a frog who could not sing but was a choirmaster. Rather than hang out with my friends during playtime, I spent most of the time imagining adventures in space, fighting aliens, and conquering colonies. I imagined I was a dashing, irresistible warrior princess with no interest in love, a superhero, a secret spy, and much more. At 11, in year 1 of Junior Secondary School, I wrote an adventure script and shared it with my friends. They loved it and pressured me to write more, but I was not ready then. As a teenager, I wanted to be a scientist and not pursue writing. I had a herbarium where I researched the flora in Abuja city and wrote a lot of research and occasional articles in local dailies. I also freelanced and edited for friends, collecting stipends in return.

I am an IT project manager, author, mother, and wife. I love studying nature, stars and their constellations, elements, history, cultures, managing complex projects, meeting people, and dancing. I am really into science fiction. I do loads of research before embarking on a writing project, and I have God as my father. I do not make assumptions about people or jump to conclusions without hearing both sides. We all have the chance to be better. My passion is writing.

I hope you enjoy reading the from my

books.

— Yemisi. Aremu Otasanya

Books By Yemisi Aremu Otasanya

 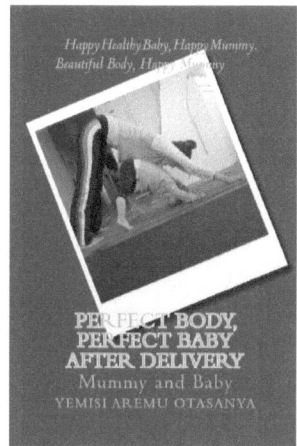